VAN2

PITTSBURGH TITANS

By
SAWYER BENNETT

Find Sawyer on the web!
sawyerbennett.com
www.twitter.com/bennettbooks
www.facebook.com/bennettbooks

Table of Contents

PITTSBURGH TIMES

THREE RIVERS SPORTING NEWS

Van Turner: A Titan Rising from Retirement

By Lisa Kuhne

From Vermont's serene landscapes, Van Turner, the former defenseman for the Carolina Cold Fury, is poised to make a dramatic comeback to the ice. The 31-year-old, who was instrumental in clinching the Cold Fury's second Cup championship three years ago, is leaving his quiet retirement to join the Pittsburgh Titans. Titans coach, Cannon West, confirmed Turner will bolster the team's defense on the third line.

Turner's story is not all ice and glory. In the midst of the Cup finals, it was revealed that he was the offspring of notorious serial killer, Arco VanBuskirk, whose life sentence ended not in parole but lung cancer two years ago. The revelation spurred speculation that Turner's retirement was a response to this unwelcome attention, but in all his press interviews, he maintained that he was content settling down with his now wife, the former Simone Fournier, starting a family and relishing his hockey achievements. The Fournier connection isn't lost on hockey fans as Simone's brothers, Lucas and Max, currently wear the Cold Fury jersey.

While it's big news that this former powerhouse of an enforcer is back on the ice, it's somewhat overshadowed by a tell-all biography recently published that delves into the chilling world of VanBuskirk, including his son's life, through a series of prison journals gifted to a reporter. Turner, who has refused so far to comment on the biography, remains a tantalizing mystery to the hockey world, but it's clear he's prepared to reenter the spotlight. The motivation behind his return may be uncertain, but what's undeniable is his resolve to leave an indelible mark on the ice once more.

CHAPTER 1

Van

I HATE THIS shit. The press is a necessary evil but I never forget it's inherently evil. I'm required by the Titans to attend this press conference held at the arena. The room hums with anticipation as I follow Coach West and our GM, Callum Derringer, through a side door and up onto a raised dais. The polished surface of the long mahogany table reflects the bright lights that illuminate the room. Three chairs are set behind it and before each chair a microphone.

The room is abuzz with chatter as the crowd engages in speculative conversation, their theories about my comeback. When we're spotted, I hear the whir of camera shutters and voices are amplified as the press poise on the edge of their seats, ready to capture the first words of this new chapter in my career.

Derringer takes the first chair, Coach West the next and I sit down on the end. Luckily, there's a swath of heavy canvas fabric pinned to the front of the table with the Titans' logo centered. It prevents anyone from seeing the nervous bounce of my leg.

Arranged in semicircular rows facing the dais are the cream of the sports press corps, armed with notepads, voice recorders and cameras, their gazes fixed on me. Some reporters are seasoned stalwarts, their faces marked by years spent under the harsh lights of arenas, while others are more wide-eyed and eager, their fingers poised above iPads to take copious notes.

On one side of the room, a sideboard holds coffee and bottled water accompanied by an assortment of pastries. On the other side, a large LED screen displays a live feed of the event for those outside the room.

Callum pulls his microphone closer and clasps his hands on the table before him as he looks out over the forty or so people in attendance. "Ladies and gentlemen, members of the press, good afternoon. As you know, I'm Callum Derringer, general manager of the Pittsburgh Titans. We're here today to welcome an extraordinary athlete back to the sport we all love, Van Turner, a man whose talent and dedication to hockey are well known and respected. We understand this is big news and want to do our best to appease your curiosity. We will only be allotting fifteen minutes, as I'm sure you can all appreciate we have to get Van on to his first practice. Please respect this time frame and make sure your questions are succinct and respectful." He pauses, surveys the rows of reporters and there's a hard glint in his eye. "We understand the high level of interest and the numerous questions you all have, but we request that you maintain a level of decorum. This is important sports news and we want to be open, but it is not a tabloid frenzy. Let's keep our focus on the sport and on the exceptional talent we're adding to our team."

A young reporter in the front stands holding a digital recorder. "It's been three years since Van Turner's retirement. What prompted the decision to bring him back into the league, especially after such a significant break and was it worth it to send Perry Veleno down to the minors as he's been putting up some impressive stats?"

Callum doesn't wait for me or Coach to weigh in, instead leaning toward the microphone. "Van Turner's legacy with the Carolina Cold Fury speaks for itself. He brings not only a wealth of experience and skill but also a unique resilience and tenacity that is the cornerstone of this new team. He aced all his strength and endurance tests, demonstrating he's still in peak condition, reinforcing our belief that his addition to the Titans will be invaluable. And I wouldn't have sent Perry Veleno down to the minors if I didn't think this was the best move for the Titans in its entirety."

The reporter lobs a follow-up. "It's one thing to maintain strength and stamina... it's another to keep your ice skills sharp."

Not a question, but an observation that still demands a response. Coach West takes it. "We did significant on-ice testing. We put Van through every skill imaginable and he's as sharp today as he was three years ago." This is true... I never left the ice, even when I retired. I played in a rec league and helped coach the Dartmouth team. "However, I think the mere fact that we signed him to a three-year contract should tell you all you need to know. We have confidence he will not only be an immediately impactful player but a long-term cornerstone for our defense."

Eager to be the next afforded the opportunity to ask a question, several are tossed out at once. Callum points and a female reporter stands. "With Van Turner joining the third line, what specific changes or improvements do you hope to see in the team's performance?"

Coach West answers. "Van's defensive abilities are top-notch. His prowess on the ice can solidify our defense, but it's his strategic understanding of the game that will help enhance our overall performance. Van's return isn't just about adding a player to our roster—it's about bringing in a seasoned professional who knows how to win and can impart that knowledge and mindset to the rest of the team. This is especially helpful since, as you know, we've rebuilt with younger players coming up from the minors."

More questions are hurled and an older reporter I

recognize from when I last played stands. He's old-school, clutching a spiral pad and pen to jot notes. His eyes come straight to me. "Van, can you comment on your father's recent biography? Has it impacted your decision to return?"

Well, that's fucking disappointing. Not that I expected the topic would be averted, but I didn't expect a veteran reporter to care about this shit. The mention of my father causes a twinge in my gut, an old wound that refuses to heal.

What I'd like to do is smash my fist into his face, but instead, I choose my words carefully. "Let's keep this about hockey. I'm here because I want to play, not to discuss a book I had no hand in writing."

The next question comes from a middle-aged man in the front row, his glasses reflecting the overhead lights. "How does your wife feel about your comeback, given her own connection to the hockey world?"

Simone.

My heart clenches at the mention of her. I wrestle with my emotions, remembering why I'm here and what I left behind. "Simone is part of the hockey community, and she understands what this life demands."

That did not answer the question, but I truly have no clue how she feels about it. I never discussed it with her. I'm surprised by how steady my voice sounds despite the fact it feels like my chest is cracking open. I glance around the room, nearly begging with my expression for someone to ask a hockey question. "Van, do you think the shadows from your past will affect your game or the Titans' dynamic?"

The pain in my chest recedes, replaced with a burning anger in my gut at the fucking idiotic question. It's a jab, trying to draw out a reaction. I force a thin smile onto my face, holding my ground. "I'm here to play hockey. I believe my skills on the ice will speak louder than any perceived 'shadows.' As for the Titans' dynamic, I'll do my part to contribute positively and play the best hockey I can."

The next few questions are focused on the training regimen I've maintained over the last three years and not on my personal life. Even though no one asks about Arco or Simone at this moment, I'm still incredibly uneasy in the spotlight. A bead of sweat rolls down my temple, but I let that be the only visible sign I'm uncomfortable. I maintain my facade, bearing the weight of my decision to step back into the public eye. After all, I'm here to play, and that's all they need to know.

"Okay... we have time for one more question," Callum says, his gaze roaming the room. A flurry of activity explodes, a disorienting storm of reporters shouting questions faster than I can process. The lights from the cameras flash relentlessly, the barrage of voices growing louder. My past, my father, my marriage... they're all on display, picked apart by these vultures.

"Van, are you afraid your father's legacy will haunt you on the ice?"

"Did Simone push you to rejoin the league?"

"What's the real reason behind your sudden return to the game?"

"Are you worried about your past distracting your teammates?"

"Did you read your father's biography?"

"Did you see your father before he died?"

The questions are painful, each one a stabbing needle of inquiry. The room spins as the noise crescendos, my heart pounding in my ears. I drop my hands to my lap so the vultures can't see me clenching my fists in anger. My skin prickles with the need to do violence because these assholes aren't here for the hockey.

They're here for the drama, for the man whose life has been a spectacle of tragedies.

I knew this was going to happen and it was still a better choice than staying with Simone. I'd rather be subjected to this every day than have another moment inside the home I built with my wife because that had become too painful to deal with.

A thunderous voice booms through the chaos. "Enough!" Callum snarls as he pounds his fist on the table, his face flushed with anger. "This is a hockey press conference, not a tabloid interrogation. If you can't keep your questions related to the game, the team or Van's professional career, you can leave."

His words hang heavy in the air, casting a noticeable chill over the reporters. The cacophony is replaced by a sudden, deafening quiet. I release a held breath, grateful for the respite.

Suddenly, the spotlight seems less glaring, the weight on my shoulders a touch lighter. But as the echoes of the questions linger, I know my fight has only just begun. I'm back in the game, back in the limelight, and now more than ever, I need to hold my ground.

"Now," Callum says, his tone calm but brooking no nonsense. "Is there one last appropriate question that someone would like to ask?"

For a moment, no one moves.

No one says a thing.

Then another female reporter stands from the back row. She looks like she just stepped out of a beauty magazine with perfect facial features and expertly coiffed hair. She must be an on-camera personality. "Van… no doubt you've followed the Titans this season. They're poised to roll into the playoffs at the top of their division. What do you think you bring to the team that could help them clinch a championship?"

Finally… a fucking question that makes sense. For the first time, my smile is genuine. "I bring experience. This team is young and while incredibly well meshed, the playoffs are an entirely different creature than the regular season. I know the stressors that come with the territory and I'm hoping more than anything to be a guide and a resource. Of course, I'm still ready to pound anyone who threatens one of my teammates."

That gets a laugh from nearly everyone and the tension in me melts a little more. Thankfully, Coach West stands up. "Unfortunately, we do have a practice to get to. Thank you everyone for attending."

I waste no time following Coach out the door, ignoring questions being yelled in the hopes I'll answer just one more.

The last one I hear before exiting hits me hard. "Van... Van... what do Lucas and Max Fournier think about your return? What will it be like battling against them?"

It's going to be a pisser because I'm sure they both want to kick my ass for what I did to Simone. Our last argument before I left home was bitter and I said hateful things to push her away. I know my barbs hit the mark because her French Canadien accent, usually so very light and melodic, had become thick from the emotion. Whereas her brothers, who had left Montreal when they were young, had all but lost their accent, Simone wore hers like a badge of armor. It was always the tell when I knew I'd really pissed her off.

But Max and Lucas are not the ones I'm worried

about. It's the youngest of the Fournier brothers, Malik, who I have to be wary of. He just happens to live here in Pittsburgh, is former Special Forces and currently works for a world-renowned security company where he's operated as a paid mercenary. He's probably got a dozen different ways to torture and make me suffer and then could easily hide my body.

I'd deserve it too.

♦

THE LOCKER ROOM is filled with the familiar post-practice symphony, and I hadn't realized how much I'd missed it until just now. The clatter of gear, the murmur of conversation, the occasional echo of laughter.

After my shower, I return to my locker, toweling my hair dry as I maneuver through.

Practice was good. Damn good, actually.

While I kept myself in shape and ran drills all the time with my league and the Dartmouth team, I did harbor a tiny bit of worry that maybe it still wouldn't have been enough to play at the professional level again. That personal concern has been put to rest and my new teammates have been offering hardy congratulations on my return.

Boone Rivers, our first-line right-winger, has his cubby next to mine. He's almost fully dressed, tugging down his T-shirt as I step up next to him. On the other side of him is Foster MacInnis, the second-line center already lacing up his shoes, his brows furrowed in concentration.

I drop my towel and reach for my clothes. Nothing strange about being butt-ass naked in front of these strangers. That's just part of the sport.

"How'd you feel out there?" Boone asks, breaking the silence between us. His voice carries a note of easy camaraderie.

"Good," I reply, casting him a glance before pulling on my boxers. "I obviously need to get up to speed on the playbook."

"You'll get there."

"It felt great to be back on the ice," I admit, donning my jeans. About the only thing worth anything I have going for me these days. "But I felt a little rusty to be playing at your level."

"You didn't look rusty," Foster chimes in, glancing up from his laces. "In fact, you looked slick as hell out there. That assist you fed me was off the hook."

"Thanks," I respond, a slight smile playing at the corners of my mouth as I treasure the thrill of the game sparking back to life within me. It burns bright against the barren emptiness.

"So, where you staying?" Foster asks as he rises from the bench and slings his duffel over his shoulder.

"Renting a place over in the Historic Mexican War Streets neighborhood. The front office had a list of places for me."

"Nice area," Foster says.

"Convenient," I reply. "It was already furnished."

"Does that mean you won't be moving your stuff from Vermont?" Boone asks.

My stomach pitches as that's getting dangerously close to a subject I don't want to talk about.

"Not anytime soon," I say vaguely as I pull my shirt over my head and then sit on the bench to put on my socks.

"Is your wife staying behind because of a job?" Foster asks genially.

The weight of the question hits harder than I expected. I swallow hard, deciding honesty is the best route. "No, she won't be joining me. We're... taking some time apart."

That's a delicate way of saying I left Simone and have no intention of reconciling with her, but I'm not about to splash my dirty laundry around.

Boone and Foster stare back at me with awkward expressions, but it's Foster who recovers first. "Ah... shit, man. I'm sorry. I wasn't being nosy or anything."

"It's cool," I say, waving a hand at him, but if he's as sensitive to my tone as I am, then he knows it's anything but.

Foster's voice drops. "I've been through it if you need to talk."

"Divorced?" I ask because that's the end goal for me, right?

"Yeah," he says with a sad shake of his head. "We have a daughter and they both live in California. You have kids?"

All I can do is shake my head, the threat of an emotional explosion nearly buckling my knees. I mean… thank fuck we don't have kids. Thank fuck Simone never got pregnant. Thank fuck that's one disaster averted.

"Not that it makes it any easier," Foster continues as he fishes in his pocket for his keys. "But still… let's get a beer sometime and commiserate."

I manage a smile, but the last thing I want to do is talk about Simone with anyone. Foster claps me on the shoulder as he moves past.

My regard cuts to Boone and I hate the sympathy on his face. I brace for him to say something about my wife, but instead, he says, "I've been hearing some of the shit in the press about your dad." My hackles rise, prepared to tell him to shut the fuck up. "Ignore that shit. Not one person on this team cares about that stuff and neither should you. It will be old news by tomorrow."

I blink in surprise, half expecting the same curiosity about my serial killer father that the reporters have. "Thanks, man."

"We got your back," he says simply, turning to his cubby.

And I have no choice but to believe it.

CHAPTER 2

Simone

STUDYING THE TWO open suitcases on my bed, I mentally calculate if I need to bring dressy clothes. On the one hand, there could be some functions that require more than jeans, cargo pants or leggings. On the other hand, even if there are team events, it's highly unlikely I'll be invited to them.

Deciding I can buy a fancy dress there if I need it, I do nothing more than toss in a pair of strappy black sandals with an incredibly high pegged heel. Those go with anything.

My phone buzzes in my back pocket causing an electrical surge of hope to zip through me, only to fizzle when I see it's my brother, Malik, texting.

Not that I don't love to hear from him, it's just that I don't particularly want to hear what he has to say today.

When are you leaving?

I glance at the suitcases, do some mental math and text back. *About half an hour.*

You're making a mistake running after him, he replies.

I move over to one of the cozy chairs set by the bedroom window and sink into it. This indeed could be a mistake. I tap my finger along the edge of my phone a few times before responding. *You'd run after Anna.*

I can envision Malik rolling his eyes and I already know the gist of his answer before it chimes its arrival. *Yeah, but she's not an asshole. Van is. Don't do it.*

Sighing, I type out my reply. *Leave it alone. He has his reasons.*

None of which are good enough.

Malik might be right about that, but I'm willing to give my husband the benefit of the doubt.

Tossing my phone on the other chair, I lean my head back and rub at my temples. I've had a perpetual headache for the last two weeks, brought on by screaming matches, bouts of painful silence, tears wept in private so he'd never see how hurt I was and the never-ending barrage of texts and calls from my brothers threatening to kill Van.

I close my eyes and try to conjure something good. It's hard to filter through all the darkness that's enshrouded my life since Arco's biography came out.

It shouldn't be difficult. Van and I have had a storybook marriage. For three years, we've lived a beautiful life in Vermont and never once did he evcr mention regret about not playing professional hockey anymore. It was his sole decision to leave after he won the Cup with the Cold Fury. He followed me north where I finished my last year of undergrad at Dartmouth, followed by a master's, and Van took classes at Green Mountain College.

He proposed.

We got married.

I became a research biologist and went to work for Dartmouth after I graduated. He joined as a coach for their hockey team. We lived, we laughed, we loved, and oh God, how we loved. Not a day passed without Van looking at me as if I'd hung the moon and the stars that went with it. Every morning I woke up giving thanks to the heavens for bringing this man into my life.

We had it so good and it got better every day... no, every minute.

The best part was just at the beginning of this year; we finally decided to get pregnant. We'd held off a few years so I could finish school and establish my career. While I was adamantly opposed to medical school, which had been my original intention to follow in my dad's footsteps, I couldn't forget that I was damn good at math and science. I didn't want to be a doctor, but I did love the thrill of research. It took me one semester to finish my undergrad and another two years to get my master's in biology. It was more than enough to make my parents proud.

Life was settled and our next big adventure was a baby.

Christ, we already fucked like rabbits and I didn't think we had any more room in our lives for sex, but Van proved me wrong. He was always pouncing on me and when he'd come deep inside me, he'd groan, "That's it, baby. Take it all from me. Let's see what we can make."

My thighs press together because that memory leaves an ache not only in the center of my chest. My eyes flutter open. I miss my husband and he's only been gone a few days. Pain lances my heart as I know he left with no intention of returning. Our last argument made it clear that my husband was broken and didn't want to be put back together.

When Arco's biography came out two weeks ago, Van spiraled rapidly. He went from horror at the revelations to anger to melancholy. I tried everything I could to reassure him, but he didn't want to hear any of it from me. He was standoffish, mean and insulting. I've seen that side of Van before, so it didn't shock me. Hell, that defined his core personality when we first met, but I was driven by the hope that I would break past those walls he erects when he's scared.

I did it once before and I could do it again. I had faith and hope and I'm relentless when I want something.

Then came the day that changed everything.

"I don't want kids," he said in the middle of an argument, and it knocked the breath out of me. Not that we'd been having sex since the book came out. That essentially killed our libidos and Van was sleeping in the guest room.

"You can't mean that," I gasped.

"I've never been more serious about anything." His glare locked on me was resolute and I heard the certainty in his voice.

"But… why?" My head was spinning. I couldn't fathom how all of our joy in creating a new life could be doused so quickly.

When he responded, it chilled my bone marrow. His tone was mocking. "Little Arco. Killer. Rapist. Freak."

"What?" I whispered, not understanding.

"That's what they called me," he sneered. "That's what little kids do when they want to be mean. That book will ensure our kids hear the same. They're going to be called names and vilified all because their father happened to be spawned by a sociopath."

"No." I shook my head adamantly. "You're wrong."

"I'm right and you know it," he said quietly.

I railed against him, using logic, pleas, tears and flat-out tantrums to get him to see he was wrong. None of it worked and finally, I capitulated and abandoned my hope of having a family with Van. I decided it would be enough for me that I have him.

I found him on the back deck after work one day. He

was drinking a beer and staring sullenly at the woods. I moved to him, draped myself over his lap and died a little inside that he wouldn't embrace me.

I put my palms to his face. "I don't need children, Van. I only need you."

I was shocked to see the look of horror on his face and he pushed up out of the chair, nearly dumping me to the ground. I scrambled from his lap and he stormed into the house. I followed, incredibly pissed.

"What the fuck, Van?" I yelled at him.

He rounded on me, pointing an accusing finger. "You're not doing that to me or yourself."

I threw my hands out in exasperation. "Doing what?"

"Denying yourself something you want or making me feel guilty about it."

"I want you!" I yelled at him. "Despite the fact you're being a fucking idiot, I want you. I'll give up kids for you. We'll be fine."

"You don't fucking get it, Simone," he bellowed, stomping over to the kitchen table. He picked up a copy of the hardback biography. I foolishly bought the damn thing so I could read it and let him know it wasn't that bad. He held it up, shook it and snarled. "This changes everything."

"It doesn't," I yelled back. "Nothing in that book touches you, Van."

The pain in his face shredded me, but then I was

terrified as he roared at me. "It doesn't just touch me, Simone. It suffocates. It kills. It annihilates."

Then he whipped the book across the living room, into the kitchen, where it crashed into a shelf of collectible mugs. They exploded, shards of pottery spraying everywhere. It was the only time Van had exhibited a violent tendency in my presence and it scared me. I took a few wary steps back.

He noticed it, too, and pounced on the meaning behind it. "See?" he growled low. "You think you know me, but maybe I'm just like Arco. Maybe I like hurting things."

It took me about half a nanosecond to understand what he was doing. He was trying to force me to abandon him and I wasn't going to do it. He tried once before and it didn't work. "You're being ridiculous," I said, crossing my arms over my chest. "Break all the damn pottery, for all I care. I'm not giving up on you. On us. We don't have to have kids."

Van sighed, raking his hand through his hair. He'd let it grow a little longer since leaving the league and I loved it. "You might not be giving up on us, but I am."

"The hell you are," I screeched. "You don't get to quit me. You know I'm a stubborn bitch, Van, and I'm never giving up on you."

Something changed in him... that very second, I saw it. I'm not sure if it was the sputtering of the flames in his eyes or the way his shoulders sagged slightly, but it scared me. "The past three years have been a farce, Simone. I'm still the same asshole you met on my front porch three years ago. I was blinded to the truth because you dazzled me so much." Van stepped into me, his expression so serious, my stomach flipped end over end. His gaze roamed my face and when it came back to lock with mine, he shook his head sadly. "You've lost your shine and I can see that very clearly now."

The tears came immediately, blurring Van's body. There were no words he could've said that would've hurt me more. It was a slap to a beautiful part of our history together.

After the first time we had sex, he tried to rebuff me and I knew it was because he was scared to develop a connection. He was such a dick and tried to scare me off by showing me just how mean he could be. "Now that you're wearing my sweat on your skin, you've sort of lost your shine. Time to move on."

That didn't hurt me then and the memory of it doesn't hurt me now.

But what tore my soul from my body when he said those words just now was because we had made a joke of it.

Me being shiny to him.

I often asked, "Am I still shiny?" and he'd always tell me I was the shiniest.

He'd often tell me that would never change. It was a promise of forever.

I cried freely, for once not hiding my sadness from my husband. Through the layer of tears, I watched as Van walked away.

Right out the front door and I heard his truck rumble out of the driveway.

He never came back.

Well… at least not when I was home. I went to work the next day, hardly able to concentrate on my projects. I pretty much spent the entire time in my head, figuring out how to make my husband see reason. By the time I left, I had resolved that this was going to be a long-haul battle and I would dig in deep. Van was not getting away from me.

Except when I got home, he shattered all of that. His drawers and closet were empty and there was a note on the kitchen table, short and to the point.

Simone,

I'm signing a contract with the Pittsburgh Titans. I'm going to find an attorney there that can help process a divorce. I'm sorry.

And that was it. The fucker didn't even bother to sign his name. I was beyond enraged when I realized he'd been planning this for a while. There's no way he just picked up the phone yesterday and found a way back into the league. His agent had to have been working on it since the book came out.

That evil asshole Arco VanBuskirk sold his life story to some gold-digging biographer and that book ruined my entire life.

It was a week ago that Van left and I haven't heard anything from him.

I claw out of the bad memories, pushing myself up from my chair. Malik is probably right. I shouldn't chase a man who doesn't want me anymore, and honestly, I'm exhausted to the bone. My husband abandoned me because he couldn't handle the hard truth of his life. It's grounds enough for divorce both legally and emotionally.

My phone buzzes, short bursts of static sounds indicating a barrage of incoming texts.

Proving that I'm still a sucker, I lunge for it, thinking it could be Van.

It's not.

Malik has now added Lucas and Max to the conversation. All three of them are hammering at me.

> **Malik:** *If you won't listen to me, maybe you'll listen to collective reasoning.*
>
> **Max:** *Baby sis… you got to let him go.*
>
> **Lucas:** *Simone's never made the best decisions, as evidenced by the fact she got caught up with him in the first place. I say we kill the motherfucker and end it now.*

Malik: *You know I can make that happen with the snap of my fingers.*

Max: *Lay off, guys… Simone's a smart woman. She'll do the right thing.*

I toss my phone and ignore their conversation. They've always been overprotective bullies when it comes to me, and if it makes them feel better to flex their brother muscles, so be it.

Sauntering into the bathroom, I transfer my toiletries to my travel case. Nothing my brothers have said has changed my mind.

And it doesn't matter that Van deserted me and is apparently getting a lawyer to file divorce papers.

I'm never fucking giving up.

Besides… my eyes drift over to the rectangular piece of plastic sitting on the vanity next to my toothbrush holder. It's been there for two days and it has become my main driving force.

I pick it up, examining the bold plus sign in the window.

"Joke's on him," I mutter and toss the positive pregnancy test in my travel bag. So much for Van deciding he doesn't want children.

CHAPTER 3

Van

A S I DRIVE home from the arena, I take stock of my emotions. Truly, I thought I'd feel different following my first game back. I skated on the third line against the Columbus Hawks and had a decent game, considering I've been out of professional play for three years. My conditioning held up and fueled by adrenaline, I wasn't as rusty as I thought I'd be. The win felt fucking good.

It's just… once I walked out of the locker room and left that all behind, the emptiness returned. Of course, I also felt empty walking into the arena and it doesn't take a genius to figure out I'm mourning the loss of Simone and the game only took my mind off things temporarily. Granted, I'm the one who cut her loose, but it doesn't mean it's not without effect.

I declined invites to join the team over at their post-game hangout place called Mario's. Despite assurances and support from the owner, team management, coaches and players, I'm too on edge over Arco's book to open myself up to anyone. I dread the inevitable questions and the risk of reporters chasing me into a bar is too real. I don't want to fucking deal with it and besides, I've never been a big people person, anyway.

At least not before Simone came into my life and now that she's gone, it took no time at all for me to regress to my surly, walled-off self. Self-preservation and being alone—this is where I feel safest.

Fucking Arco.

I've never felt actual hate toward a single person, but I feel it pulsing throughout me every time I think about him. If he weren't dead already and I could get away with it, I'd murder him in cold blood without a single ding to my conscience. He was pure evil, a sociopath who thrived on not only raping and killing but on torturing his son after it was all said and done.

I visited Arco three years ago—ironically after Simone and I had been intimate for the first time. He had lung cancer and was dying. I was a glutton for punishment, so I went to see him. Not because I loved him and not because I needed to make my peace with all the heinous things he'd done.

I needed to know if I was anything like him. Three days after he was convicted and sent to prison, my mother killed herself. She couldn't handle the truth and took a handful of pills, knowing I'd be the one to find her body. It was my aunt, Etta Turner, who whisked me away to California, changed my name from Grant VanBuskirk to Van Turner, and helped me start fresh. I grew up away from the spotlight, hidden behind a new name and a new mom.

But I never forgot my dad or the horrific things he did to women. And I knew all the gory details since my mom forced me to sit through his entire trial at the tender age of eight. I never stopped wondering if I was anything like him since his DNA gave me his physical features. We looked a lot alike, and I was terrified my insides matched his.

That visit confirmed we were nothing alike. He was a self-centered, cruel narcissist who tried to torture me emotionally during that very short visit. I left with all my questions answered and wiped my hands clean of him.

Of course, Arco wasn't done with me. He spilled my true identity to an independent reporter who wrote a hack piece opining that I was probably as crazy as my sire. It nearly destroyed me that my shameful secret was revealed to the world and I almost lost Simone because I reacted badly to it. I tried to push her away and crawl back into my fortress of solitude. Luckily, I quickly realized my mistake and rectified it.

Fortunately, Simone is a forgiving woman who loves me to the depths of her soul.

Sucks that it's not enough this time, because when that tell-all biography came out, it sealed my future.

While I could reason with myself that with Arco dead all the sordid details of what he did and the interest in it would fade away, the fact that the biography hit the *New York Times* bestseller list ensured it would never go to the grave. I was always going to have to deal with it and if it was just me, fine… I'd deal.

But now it was going to follow Simone and haunt our children. The thought of my kids suffering the same abuse and bullying I did simply by being related to Arco was untenable. That book ensured I would never procreate and put anyone else in harm's way to suffer Arco's sins.

I'd probably stay immersed in these wretched loops of painful memories if not jolted by the car parallel parked in front of my house. Normally, I'd drive right by, turn down the next street and loop into the back alley where my garage sits, but the green Vermont license plate catches my attention first, followed by the immediate recognition of Simone's BMW.

My head swivels to see her sitting on my front stoop, the porch light illuminating her clearly. She doesn't see me, head bowed over her cell phone. She has three pieces of luggage sitting beside her.

"Fuck," I growl, slamming on the brakes and leaving rubber on the asphalt.

Her head pops up to lock eyes with me through the passenger window. There's no mistaking the stiffening of her shoulders or the wariness in her expression. I'm sure she can see I'm pissed, but even as angry as I am she followed me here, I can't say I'm surprised.

It was probably expected and I refuse to let myself admire her for it. Her tenacity and sheer bullheadedness are two of the reasons I was so attracted to her when we first met.

Shifting into reverse, I whip into the spot right behind her and exit my truck. I round the back end, cross over the sidewalk and come to stand at the base of the stairs.

"What the hell are you doing here?" I snarl, hoping to scare her into submission. "And how the hell did you even find me?"

"Malik," she says. Of course it would be Malik. He works for a company that can locate anyone in the world. Hell, they located him when he'd been kidnapped in Syria and held prisoner in a hole in the middle of the desert for months.

"You need to go," I say, pointing back at her car.

"Nope."

"Goddamn it, Simone. You're not welcome here."

"I'm married to you and any home you live in is considered marital property, so I'm allowed to be here as much as you are."

That's bullshit and she knows it.

"And what are you hoping to accomplish?" I ask,

throwing my arms out in confusion. "Other than pissing me off."

"I like pissing you off," she says as she rises and dusts off the back of her jeans. "And I'm here to make you see reason. I'm getting you back."

I scrub my hands over my face, at a loss for what to do or say.

"If you wanted to play professional hockey again, why didn't you just tell me?" Simone asks softly, and I'm knocked off-kilter by that question. "I would have supported you. I would have uprooted myself in a nanosecond to let you pursue that dream."

Christ, I know she would and it's why I love her so much. But I'm not about to tell her that. "I didn't tell you because coming back into the league was my escape plan. I didn't want you to follow me."

Hurt flashes in her beautiful hazel eyes. "That's cruel."

"I told you before that I wasn't a nice man and that I was going to hurt you one day."

"I remember. And you did hurt me once and I forgave you for it. I'm going to forgive you for this as well. Just out of curiosity, how long had you been planning this escape from me back into the league?"

"The day the book came out," I admit truthfully. When a reporter called to ask me about it, and I realized what was happening, I called my agent that very same day. I knew right then that I would never drag kids through this and I'd have to cut Simone loose so she could live her dreams.

Simone crosses her arms over her chest. "You should have just left that day, then. It would've been a lot easier."

"I know," I mutter. "I'm kicking myself."

"A lot easier on me, you asshole," she barks, marching down the steps to come toe to toe with me. She has to tip her head back to see my face. "I don't care if it's hard on you. In fact, I don't believe it is hard on you. You don't seem to give two shits that you're ending our marriage. You don't care that you've hurt me."

My hand flies out so fast, she squeaks with fright. I grasp her around the back of her neck and pull her in closer. "Don't ever say I don't care about you. It's because I care I'm doing this."

That earns me a solid punch to my stomach and it hurts enough I release her. She steps in closer, pokes a finger in my chest. "You're a moron and a coward. But that's okay. You used to be that way once and I managed to turn you around. I'll do it again."

"Jesus Christ, you're fucking nuts, Simone," I yell at her. "Why can't you just accept this and be done with it?"

"Because I'm not a quitter," she seethes. "I'm back in your life and I'm going to do whatever I can to get your head out of your ass."

"F-u-u-u-c-k!" I bellow, clasping my hands on top of my head. I'm so pissed I think it might explode. I take in her resolute stare and cannot even deal with her. I brush past her, jogging up the steps with my keys in hand.

She follows behind me and when we reach the top, I spin and put my hand out to stop her trajectory. It presses into her chest and I hold her at arm's length. "I don't want you here."

"Too bad. I'm your wife and you love me."

"I don't want you anymore."

"Liar," she retorts.

She's infuriating and so fucking stubborn that I have to resort to cruelty. "I don't love you, Simone. Not enough to work this out."

"Such a liar," she says as she smacks my hand away and moves to the door. "Get my bags, will you?"

"No way. You are not staying here. Go to Malik's house."

Challenge and a devious glint spark in her eye and my pulse skitters with dread. Simone knows how to get her way. "What's wrong, Van? Afraid of me? Afraid your resolve might not be that strong? That you can't hold up against me? I toppled you once and it wasn't that hard."

Okay, now that just affronts me on a competitive level. It's true that Simone was like a dog with a bone when she came after me before, but she has no clue the level of sincerity or deep belief I have that I'm doing the right thing.

I don't take the bait. Instead, I say, "I'm giving you about thirty seconds to clear off my porch or I'm calling the police to say you're trespassing."

"You call the police and I'm calling every news agency in Pittsburgh to have them record the police removing me from my own home. I'm sure they're going to love hearing the entire story of how you're abandoning me because of some stupid book."

Rage flashes hot through me from my complete loss of control. I wouldn't put it past Simone to do just such a thing.

My mind spins. The woman is absolutely too fucking tenacious. When she set her sights on me, she poked at me over and over again, impervious to my insults to get her to back away.

Simone knew no bounds and had no shame. She moved in without an invitation to the house I was sharing with her brother, Lucas, and immediately decided she wanted me. Provocation was her game and she stepped over boundaries whenever she felt like it.

Once she came into my bedroom.

"What the fuck are you doing in here?" I snarled.

She pursed those utterly kissable lips. "Just trying to get to know you. You make it kind of hard, you know."

"I don't want to know you. I'm a temporary roommate

to your brother. You're just a houseguest."

She pouted and I had a million dirty fantasies about that mouth. "Now that just hurts my feelings."

"Apparently not enough to drive you out of my room, though," I snapped.

"Come on, Van." She tried for a begging tone, but I could tell that woman begged for nothing. "Give me a shot. I make a fun friend, and if you're interested in a benefits package with that friendship, I'm fucking dynamite in the sack."

I was stunned stupid. "You did not just say that to me."

She batted her eyelashes. "Why not? It's the twenty-first century. Believe it or not, women have a firm grip on their sexuality. Some of us even—and don't get too bent out of shape about this—actually like to have sex."

I felt like I was in a bad dream, unable to come up with a good comeback, and on top of that, my dick twitched.

"I really, really like to have sex," she added. "And you look like you'd be fantastic at it. I mean… I'm fantastic. I'm also quite bendy in bed. My flexibility is—"

My dick more than twitched, it started to swell and I bolted from my room. Six foot six of solid muscle and meanness out on the ice and I was running from her.

The more Simone rattled me, the harder she came at me. The harder she came at me, the easier I wore down until she provoked me into action. Forced me to acknowledge the boiling lust for her and I took what she offered.

That changed the entire trajectory of my life. Led me to my greatest love.

And now, my greatest loss.

I cannot go back there again. It was too hard walking away from her last week.

But it's suddenly clear to me what I need to do. Telling her to leave and spewing lies that I don't love her will not do the trick. They'll just make her double down.

No... I need to do something different. Something that will frustrate her to no end and will have her running sooner rather than later.

I'm going to ignore her.

Turning my back, I unlock the door and enter my house. She scrambles in after me, assuredly afraid I'll try to lock her out.

I don't. Merely toss my keys on the small table by the door and disable the alarm at the wall panel. I unbutton my suit jacket. I hadn't bothered with an overcoat because the short walk through the players' lot in the arena garage didn't warrant it.

"What are you doing?" she asks hesitantly, but I don't look back at her.

"Going to bed," I reply as I move through the living room.

"Aren't you going to help me with my bags?"

"Nope." I stop at the edge of the hallway that leads

to the first-floor master. I jerk my head to the staircase. "There's a guest room up there."

"You want me to sleep in the guest room?"

"I don't give a fuck what you do, Simone. But there are a few rules if you stay here."

"What's that?" she snaps, irritation written all over her beautiful face.

"Don't come near me. Don't talk to me."

She scoffs because I can already tell she's deviously brainstorming ways around that. "Is that all?"

"You're a roommate. Nothing more. I expect you to have a care for this house and my personal property inside of it. As such, don't you dare leave it without locking it tight and entering the alarm code."

"Fine. Give me a key and the code."

I shake my head, leveling her with a viciously triumphant smile. "Yeah, that's not happening."

"Then how do you expect me to come and go?" she asks.

"Not my problem. Preferably, you would just go, but if you're going to pursue this stupid idea of brow-beating me into getting back with you, I don't have to stick around. I plan on being out of this house as much as possible and you'll just have to stay behind to make sure it's safe."

"I won't be kept prisoner," she says with confidence.

"You won't risk someone stealing things that are

36

important to me. You won't risk someone stealing your stuff. So I'm guessing you'll stay put."

She rolls her eyes. "You know this is so childish."

I lift a shoulder. "Just establishing clear lines. Stay on your side, okay?"

I can see she's flummoxed and a thrill sweeps through me that I have the upper hand. She chews on her bottom lip, her gaze darting around, trying to figure out how to get back on top. I'll let her stew on it in private.

Smiling to myself, I head into the master bedroom and lock the door behind me.

CHAPTER 4

Simone

"**T**HIS IS COMPLETELY stupid, Simone."

I glance from the kitchen table over to the front door where Malik is installing a new alarm panel. My attention slides back to Anna sitting across from me and she grins in amusement. He's been grumbling since he got here over an hour ago to change the locks and alarm panel.

Malik isn't happy I'm not staying with him and Anna. Of course, he's not happy I'm pursuing my husband, but he's never going to deny me the chance to pursue my dreams.

And Van is my dream.

"You know he can just get these changed again," Malik says as he bends over a laptop resting on the arm of the couch.

"He won't," I say with the utmost confidence. I know Van well. This will piss him off, frustrate him to no end, but he won't bother changing it back. He knows I'll just change it back again and he doesn't have the time or energy to battle me on this.

Part of me feels guilty as I'm not doing this to make him mad or even to poke him into dealing with me. I simply can't be constrained to the house. I need to be able to run errands, see my brother and go to a Titans game to root for my husband. I can't be a prisoner.

Anna shakes her head as her fingers play with the rim of her coffee cup. "I still don't understand how it came to this."

I love my sister-in-law very much, just as I love Malik. But as much as I love them, I love Van more and I'll never divulge his secrets. His terror and shame stemming from Arco's biography is private. It's not something he's asked me to keep to myself, but it is the deepest, most intimate part of himself he's shared with me. While most of this has come in the form of arguments, it's still protected information.

I can only give them a vague idea, so I choose my words carefully. "Van struggles with the stigma attached to his dad. He's afraid of the repercussions."

"He needs to man the fuck up," Malik mutters.

My head whips his way and I glare at my brother, completely defending my husband. "Not repercussions to himself, you dumbass. To me."

And to our unborn children, but that isn't something I'm going to divulge either. We didn't tell anyone we were trying to get pregnant. We didn't want the pressure of others impatiently waiting for it to happen.

"But surely he knows you don't care about that," Anna says, drawing my attention back to her.

"He knows," I reply, picking up my cup to take a sip. "But *he* cares and that's all that matters to him."

"He pulled this shit with you three years ago when that first article came out," Malik says, turning toward the panel where he pushes some buttons. "And you didn't stick around to put up with it. You left and he came groveling after you. I don't understand why you're the one chasing when he's being the same dick."

Because it's different. Because babies are involved, or at least the hope of babies, and Van can't see past the horror.

"It's not your place to judge his feelings," I tell my brother, and I see his shoulders sag a little. "It's not your place to judge how I'm handling this."

He glances back at me. "I'm not. I just love you and don't want you hurt again."

"I'm already hurt," I admit candidly. Malik curses under his breath. "But I'm going to let Van fix it. Now, let's talk about something else."

God, please let this be fixed.

Malik nods and goes back to work. Anna taps the table to get my attention. "Your brother and I are embarking on a new adventure."

"Oh, really," I say, propping my chin in my palm.

"Tell me all."

"We're trying to get pregnant," she squeaks with excitement.

I manage a brilliant smile as I force back the overwhelming sadness that I used to be just as excited at the prospect of getting pregnant. Only a few weeks ago, I would've been screaming it at the top of my lungs, but now it's my secret to bear until I can knock some sense into my husband.

"Yay!" I yell and reach for her hand. "I'm going to be an auntie again."

Anna already has a daughter named Avery from a former marriage. Her husband Jimmy died while on a mission with Malik. Anna went through that birth alone, and Malik was captured and held prisoner for months. When he returned, somewhat a shell of the man he once was, it was Anna who brought him back to life. They fell in love and got married. Just last month, Malik formally adopted Avery, but they decided to leave her last name as Tate rather than change it to Fournier, to honor her father.

I sit back and listen to Anna gush about their decision while Malik finishes up at the alarm panel. When he comes to the table, he bends over Anna and kisses the top of her head. My heart squeezes because while Van has touched me a million different ways, one of my favorites was just a gentle touch in passing.

Malik goes to the fridge and pulls out a beer. Holding it up, he says, "At least Van's good for something."

I don't bother chastising him. He's never going to not be mad at Van and I can only hope that when I repair my marriage, my brothers will forgive him.

When he plops down in the chair next to me, he asks, "What the hell are you doing about your job? Did they give you an extended vacation or something?"

I shake my head. "I'll work remotely."

"You can do that?" Anna asks.

"For a while. I'll be working on mostly data analysis and report writing based on studies carried out by on-site teams."

"And what's the current project, Miss Smartest Fournier Sibling?" Malik queries.

I snicker because my brothers may not have gone to college but they are all as bright as I am. "We're assessing the impact of acid rain in the New England forest ecosystems."

Malik cocks a brow. "There's acid rain in New England?"

I pat him on the arm. "Hate to tell you, big bro, but there's acid rain around any areas that have sulfur- and nitrogen-emitting industries."

"Like the type that will melt your skin?"

Laughing, I shake my head. "You watch too many sci-fi movies. No, acid rain is far too weak to burn skin, but it is hell on the ecosystem."

"And that's why you're the brainiac in the family," he says, raising his beer in silent toast. His smile slides, though. "But seriously… come stay with me and Anna. I'm totally fine if you want to try to work things out with Van, but I know this is hard. You should be around people who love you."

"I am," I reply simply. "Van hasn't stopped loving me. In fact, he thinks that this is the right thing to do because he loves me."

"Fucking moron," Malik mutters.

Not going to disagree with him there. "I know what I'm doing. Just support me while I do this, okay?"

"Fine," he says, holding up a hand in capitulation. "But promise you will spend time with us."

"That is a promise I can absolutely make."

"And when Lucas and Max come week after next, we'll figure a way we can all get together."

That would be awesome. I don't know how their schedule will pan out if they're doing an overnight or an out-and-back when they come to play the Titans, but at the very least, we'll manage to hang for a bit. At least that gives me something to look forward to.

♦

I'M SITTING AT the kitchen table, working on my laptop, when I hear Van slip his key into the door. I stand up and walk that way because his key no longer works. He was gone when I woke up this morning, and it's nearly nine p.m. He said he was going to be gone as much as possible to avoid me and I should feel guilty about it, but I don't. I don't intend to make this comfortable for him.

The knob jiggles and then he bangs on the door.

I open it and step back.

"Why the hell doesn't my key work?" he fumes, but I can see by the look on his face, he knows.

I nod to the small table to the new spare sitting there. "There's your key and the new alarm code is 5683. It spells LOVE, in case you forget."

Van curses but I turn away and walk into the kitchen. I don't look back at him but I can hear his keys jangling, so I know he's switching out the old for the new.

"Did you eat dinner?" I ask pleasantly. "I made salad and baked chicken. It's in the fridge."

Van doesn't look at me or answer my question. I log out of the Dartmouth portal after saving my work and shut my laptop.

Opening the fridge, he pulls out a beer, twists off the cap and throws it in the sink, done specifically to annoy me, I'm sure. He takes three long pulls from the brew and then rummages through a cabinet, pulling out a can of soup. I watch as he pulls the top off the can and eats it cold with a spoon.

Ignoring me.

Refusing to eat perfectly good food I prepared.

"I'm done with my work," I say, an innocuous attempt at conversation. "My boss is going to let me project manage remotely until we can figure out how to fix things."

Van doesn't even flinch, concentrating on his icy chicken noodle while leaning against the counter. He stares blankly ahead.

I wonder what he'd do if I just blurted out to him that I'm pregnant. Just to get a reaction from him because this patent ignoring me is grating on my nerves. I don't do it, though, because I am never going to use this baby as leverage. I don't want him beholden to me in any way. I'd rather be a single mom than force him into a lifelong commitment with me that he doesn't want.

Van tosses the empty soup can in the garbage, the spoon in the sink without even rinsing it, and I have to restrain myself not to get up and do it. He walks back into the living room and settles in the middle of the couch, resting the beer on the coffee table. Grabbing the remote control, he turns on the TV and flips through the channels.

I grit my teeth when I see him land on a reality TV show about three mechanic brothers who refurbish old cars. They're obnoxious loudmouths who make crude jokes and belittle people. Van watches it for the cars, but I want to scratch my eyes out and pour acid in my ears when it's on. Back home, he'd only ever watch it if I was busy doing something else. He would laugh at me—my hatred of the show—but he never subjected me to it. Just like I never subjected him to my obsession with *The Bachelor*.

His intention to drive me away made clear, I push up out of the chair and walk through the living room. I cross right in front of the TV and watch him carefully. He doesn't let his attention focus on me at all.

He thinks by ignoring me, I'll go away. He thinks by failing to engage with me, I'll leave him alone.

Yeah… he's wrong about that.

I walk up the stairs with purpose. I slept in one of the guest rooms last night. It had no linens on the bed, so I made do with a blanket I found in one of the closets. But if I'm in that room, I can't be near Van, so things will need to change.

CHAPTER 5

Van

I WATCH SIMONE as she heads up the stairs and fucking everything on my body clenches tight. My fists because I'm angry, my body because watching her ass sway as she takes the steps is killing me and my heart because everything is all fucked up.

This was supposed to be a clean break and she's making a mess of everything.

Rationally, I understand my wife doesn't want our marriage to end. I even believe her without reservation when she says she can handle the nasty fallout from Arco's book. But I can't go through watching her or any potential children suffer. I'm protecting her the best way I can and that's by breaking away from her life so she can go on to find someone to love her—never as much as I do—but who can give her a beautiful life with beautiful kids who will never have a moment of this ugliness in their lives.

Leaning forward, I pick up my beer and bring it to my mouth, but it freezes halfway as I hear Simone coming down the stairs. I settle back onto the couch, rest the bottle on my thigh and laser my attention to my show.

She moves in front of the TV and once she's passed, I permit myself to look at her.

Jesus fucking Christ!

I have to suppress a groan and order my dick to behave. Simone's wearing next to nothing—just a tight white tank top with spaghetti straps and a pair of white bikini panties. Her ass is slamming, her tits full and nipples pushing through the fabric. I wonder if the little minx played with them upstairs to get them hard to grab my attention. There's no doubt in my mind this little display of near-nakedness is part of the war she's waging.

If it was just her wearing skimpy clothes I could probably deal but I'm confused by the fact she's carrying a blanket, a pillow and a small tote bag, so I continue to watch.

Rounding the coffee table, she moves to the end of the couch and tosses the pillow and blanket there before resting the tote on the floor.

I hate to break my self-imposed silence but I can't help but ask, "What are you doing?"

Her gaze lifts. "I'm going to sleep on the couch tonight."

"Why?"

She proceeds to fluff the pillow and spread the blanket. I slide to the far end of the couch away from her. My move amuses her as evidenced by her husky laugh. "I'm going to recreate how it was when we first met. You tried to ignore me and I was sleeping on the couch."

Simone flips the blanket back and slides onto the cushion. She extends her legs and I scramble off before her feet touch me.

"So jumpy," she coos and makes no effort to cover herself with the blanket. Smooth-as-silk legs with red painted toenails and my heart fucking thumps hard. I hate being attracted to her so much.

I settle into a corner chair, refusing to be forced out of the room. I intend to sit here, watch my crappy TV show she hates and completely ignore her so she can see she has no effect. Although, admittedly, the way I jumped away from her was a point in her favor.

I sip my beer, settle the bottle back on my leg and try to focus on the TV. But from the corner of my eye, I see Simone lean over to rummage through the tote she brought down. I cut a glance at her to see she's pulled out a bottle of lotion, and not just any lotion. A special brand that I buy her that smells like cherry blossoms.

Putting my focus back on the television, I hear the click of the bottle opening and I can see her moving, rubbing lotion on her legs and arms. The sweet scent reaches my nose and fuck if that doesn't make my dick take notice.

She's a witch and she knows all the subtle ways to seduce.

"Can I ask you a question?" she asks.

I refuse to look at her. Refuse to answer.

Simone sighs. "I just want to know if you'd have sex with me tonight."

There's no stopping my head from turning her way. "What?"

"Sex. I want to have sex with you. I miss having sex with you. So will you?"

Yes!

"No." My head swings back to the TV, but it's not enough to just deny her. I need to start breaking down this eternal optimism she has for us. "Besides, I told you before... you lost your shine."

"*No* would have sufficed," she pouts. "You don't have to be a jerk."

"Apparently, I do," I mutter before taking a long pull on my beer.

She doesn't reply, doesn't move. Several minutes go by before she lets out another sigh and then reaches over to her tote. I refuse to peek but from the periphery, I can see she grabbed something from the bag and she settles back onto the couch.

A buzzing sound fills the air and it forces me to look at her, my curiosity just too fucking sensitive.

My jaw drops when I see she's got a vibrator in her

hand. Purple, about six inches in length and a fairly thick girth. I know it well because I bought it for her probably a year ago and I use it on her from time to time. She runs the tip of it casually along the top of her thigh, then back down again, her eyes pinned to it.

"You know," she says softly, her gaze lifting to meet mine—assured I'll be watching. "I'd really love to crawl on my hands and knees to you. I'd kill to take you in my mouth. I'd make you see stars, baby." The fingers on my free hand curl into the chair's upholstery. "But I know you don't want me like that since I'm not shiny anymore." Simone changes the trajectory of the vibrator and it slides along the inside of her leg where she rubs it along her panty line. "Guess I'll just have to take care of myself."

My cock swells to aching proportions and I cannot stop watching her. She lets her legs fall open, uses her delicate fingers to pull her panties to the side so she can—

I lunge out of the chair, spilling my bottle of beer and cracking my knee on the coffee table. I abandon the beer and try not to hobble through the living room and down the hall to the master bedroom.

I slam the door behind me, locking it for good measure because Simone can't be trusted. I pace with agitation. Christ, she knows how to rile me up, and there is nothing in this world I want more than to go back out there, put her across my lap and blister her backside with my palm before fucking her hard. It's what she wants me to do. It's what she's goading me to do.

I hear something and freeze.

Was that laughter? She'd have every right to be amused over my hasty retreat and I'll let her have this joke because she played that perfectly.

I tip my head but I can't tell exactly what I'm hearing. Ever so carefully to not make any noise and with much thanks that this house was recently renovated so there are no squeaky hinges, I unlock the door and ease it open just an inch.

The soft sounds of weeping reach me and it feels like my chest cracks right down the middle. Out of all the fights we've had the last few weeks, Simone has held a stiff upper lip. She only cried once and that was the day I left, although I suspect she might have done so in private. She's a proud woman and likes to be strong.

The desolation within her soft sobs makes me question what kind of monster I am. Because no matter how much it kills me that I've hurt her, I'm not changing my mind about anything.

Quietly, I shut my door again and lock it.

Moving to the bed, I sit on the edge and open the drawer of the bedside table. I pull out the thick hardback book. The dust jacket is bright white and on the front is a black-and-white picture of my father. The publisher chose to go with a candid taken during his trial. It was of him sitting at the defendant's table, leaning back in his chair to talk to me and my mother as we sat in the front row. My stomach cramps seeing eight-year-old me sitting there, in my Sunday suit with my hair slicked down. I look terrified and out of place. My dad is smiling, holding hands with my mom, propped on the low wall that separates the front of the courtroom from where the public sits. He does not look like a man on trial for multiple rapes and murders but rather a good father and husband who has been separated from his family.

Nausea wells and bile surges up my throat as I read the title of the book. "*Chip Off the Old Block.*"

I don't know how much input Arco had into this book. I only know he sold his prison diaries to a biographer, but the title is a direct message to me.

When I visited my father in prison before he died, he knew exactly why I was there and he played right into my fears. Arco sat across from me, thick, bulletproof glass separating us. We communicated through a phone, but it didn't lessen the crudity of his words.

"My jizz is what knocked up your bitch of a mother," he told me with an evil glint in his eye. "You got my fucking DNA, boy. You're my son no matter what some paper says. A regular chip off the old block."

It's what he used to say to me growing up. Arco wasn't a tender man and he didn't believe in hugs or cuddles. He was funny, gregarious and everyone loved him. But he never told me he loved me and he never hugged me. That's because he had no conscience and no capacity to love.

He could only deceive.

And murder and rape.

Arco used words carefully and when he called me a "chip off the old block," he did it with intent. When I was little, I only wanted his pride in me and I'd beam when he declared such. Now it makes me physically sick to think of his DNA coursing through my body.

I'm wondering why the biographer focused on that phrase. It was clearly in the diaries and perhaps my dad wrote about that last encounter between us. Maybe he had a good laugh over how easy it was to terrify his grown son who was a big, tough hockey player.

My fingers play at the edge of the book. I want to read it, but I haven't been able to bring myself to do it. I know Simone bought a copy and she read it.

"It's nothing but drivel, Van," she had said with a wave of her hand, like it was nothing more than a nuisance, like a gnat buzzing around her head. "The biographer didn't do much other than regurgitate Arco's words with bad literary prose and he comes off like the lunatic he was. None of it's credible."

I didn't have the guts to ask her what it said about me and she didn't offer. I think she figured I'd never read it and what I didn't know couldn't hurt me.

Taking a deep breath, I open the cover of the book and stare blankly at the title page. My hand shakes as I grab a chunk of pages and start flipping, not with any real intention of reading anything. It's a victory just opening the book.

But a phrase catches my attention as a chapter header whizzes by and I stop, flip back to the spot.

Chapter 5: Unveiling Shadows

I skim the first few paragraphs and realize it's about me. Or rather, Arco's reflections about his only son who was called Grant VanBuskirk at the time.

I think I might vomit and my brain is telling me to slam the book shut. I think of the weeping woman on the other side of the door who doesn't think this is a big deal.

That I can persevere.

I inhale deeply, blowing out slowly.

Try to calm the frantic racing of my pulse.

I focus on the words and start reading.

Within the faded pages of Arco's diaries lay a chilling chronicle of his observations on Grant, his son. The entries, devoid of warmth or remorse, offered a disconcerting glimpse into the mind of a convicted serial killer. Veiled within these revelations, the secrets of Grant's young existence came to light, raising unsettling questions about the twisted threads of their shared bloodline.

Through the prism of Arco's warped perspective, a peculiar essence emerged—the contours of Grant's character and a sincere desire that his son have the same unnatural detachment that made him a sociopath.

Arco found himself captivated by his son's unquenchable curiosity, recognizing in it a familiar hunger for exploration. At the tender age of six, Grant's quest for knowledge surpassed mere childhood inquisitiveness, evoking memories of his father's own sinister proclivities.

I try to suck in a breath, but there's no air in my lungs. What the fuck is he inferring?

Among the haunting tales, one incident loomed over their shared history. Grant's encounter with a delicate bird's nest concealed within their backyard sent ripples of unease through the mind that penned these unsettling memoirs. Instead of a passive appreciation of its fragile beauty, Arco writes how Grant succumbed to what he called a "predatory instinct." It welled Arco with pride when his son's innocent hands closed around the unborn lives within. For Arco, it was a chilling reflection, a confirmation of a dark legacy he had unknowingly bestowed upon his son.

From behind prison bars, Arco reveled in the twisted possibilities. The notion of Grant carrying forth his father's malevolence, of mastering the art of manipulation, ignited a nefarious pride within him. His imagination wove intricate narratives within his diaries where Grant's path intertwined with his own, both predator and prey, mirroring each other's dark desires.

In this enigmatic dance of nature and nurture, the omniscient observer glimpsed the blurred lines of Grant's fate. Would he succumb to the haunting allure of his lineage, embracing the legacy of darkness that coursed through his veins? Or would he defy the shackles of his bloodline, forging a path untainted by the sins of his father?

Jesus!

Fuck!

The book falls from my hands, thudding to the carpet. I lurch off the bed and stagger into the bathroom. Falling to my knees, I barely get the toilet cover opened before I vomit. The beer comes up mixed with the soup, splashing in the toilet bowl. My stomach empty, I continue to wretch as the words I just read reverberate through me.

Panic starts to overwhelm me and it feels like a cinder block is on my chest. I try to drag in a deep lungful of air to break the claustrophobia of my anxiety, but I'm only able to pant through the terror of it all.

I push away from the toilet bowl and sag against the shower door. Something tickles my cheek and I reach up, realizing my face is wet with tears.

That fucker lied. I had no such predatory instinct and I most certainly never tried to destroy those bird's eggs. I was so excited to find them and I showed my mother. I wanted to touch one, but she wouldn't let me. Arco was sitting on the patio, drinking a beer and watching us.

And that was it.

That's all that happened, but he portrayed me as having the same dark desires he had.

He's a sociopath, I remind myself.

Rather, his official diagnosis was antisocial personality disorder.

Among its many characteristics are manipulation and lying for personal gain.

All of it is a big fucking lie and yet… it's been printed. It's in the hands of thousands upon thousands of people. News channels are discussing it, reporters are calling me to get my side.

Because they fucking want to believe that I crush eggs with baby birds inside.

I rub my hands over my face and when I open my eyes, they land on the book lying just past the bathroom door on the carpet.

There's no way Simone read this book because if she'd read just that one passage, she'd be running as far away from me as possible.

My resolve is renewed. Simone can't be a part of my life. She doesn't deserve the fetid stink of Arco's legacy and all I can think is, *Thank fuck we didn't get pregnant.*

CHAPTER 6

Simone

THE ZOOM MEETING is wrapping up and I share my screen with the team. "If you'll look at the spreadsheet, I've broken down this week's collections prospects. Hardy's team will handle soil, water and foliar samples. Renshaw will do the insects and invertebrates."

"Bug dude," someone calls out, but I don't know who.

Several people laugh and Renshaw says, "Can't help it if you scientists are too weenie to catch and dissect the critters."

Ordinarily, I would laugh and give everyone else hell about it, but nothing seems funny anymore. I plow right along. "Farber's team is on lichens and tree core samples. Any questions?"

Of course there are and I weed through them one by one. Ordinarily, if I were back home, I'd be on one of the collection teams as we work on the acid rain project and then I'd have my face pressed to a microscope, which is my favorite part of what I do. But now I'm doing mostly project management and data analysis as I work from Pittsburgh.

"If you can have results to me in ten days, that would be good. Any more questions?"

Blessedly, there aren't any and I sign off after good-byes where I paste a smile on my face. Once the camera's off, I rub my eyes. They're sore and gritty from a combination of crying and not sleeping well. I've been here in Van's home going on my fifth day now and he hasn't spoken a word to me in four. Granted, he's been on a road trip to Los Angeles the last two days and is coming back tomorrow, but I don't know the details because he hasn't shared them with me. My texts go unanswered and the only way I knew he was traveling for games was to look up the actual team schedule online.

He's so fucking frustrating and I'm running out of ideas. All my attempts to provoke him go unanswered. He's mastered the ability to ignore and avoid, often staying away from the house until it's time to go to bed and then leaving first thing in the morning. I'm still sleeping on the couch, just so I can catch a glimpse of him. I cook every night but he refuses to eat my food.

I'm lonely and miserable and about to give up. Last night I went over to Anna and Malik's house because the isolation is getting to me. I knew I'd have to hear Malik's disgruntlement over my attempts to get Van turned around, but it was worth it to have some company.

"Jesus, you look like shit, Simone," he'd said when he opened the door and just before pulling me into him for a hug.

"Feel like it too," I admitted as I ran my fingers through my hair. It hit on tangles and I wasn't even sure I'd brushed it after my shower that morning.

Anna was next to hug me as she held Avery on her hip, and then I pulled my niece away from her because kids always make me happy.

But it also made me sad, too, because I'm starting to understand that Van probably isn't going to be a part of our baby's life. It's one of only a million worries I have about being pregnant and the current state of disaster that is our marriage. It's been weighing on me so heavily that I also broke down last night and told Anna.

It was a spur-of-the-moment decision and I probably wouldn't have done it had Van at least been engaging me somewhat. But I'm overwhelmed by the solitude and desperation, and I need someone to understand fully what's going on with me. While I love Malik to the moon and back, I needed a woman on my side.

Malik had gone to put Avery down to sleep and I purged everything to Anna. Her eyes got wider and wider and nearly bugged out when I told her I was pregnant, but God, it felt good to let that secret out. We didn't have much time to talk about it because Malik would be returning shortly, but she hugged me hard and promised she had my back. I extracted a promise from her not to tell Malik and she had no qualms about it.

"Have you seen a doctor yet to find out how far along you are?" she asked, and I nearly burst into tears.

I admitted that I didn't want to go until Van could be by my side.

But the likelihood of that happening is looking more remote by the day. Sighing, I push the kitchen chair back from the table and rise. My back is killing me as I've been up working since six a.m., nearly three hours in that hard, wooden chair without a break.

I stare longingly at the coffee pot. I've had to cut that out since finding out I was pregnant and I miss caffeine like I'd miss air if I were underwater. That's especially so since I'm functioning on only a few hours of sleep each night.

Maybe I'll go for a walk. It's nearly fifty degrees out today, which is practically balmy coming from Vermont where it's a good fifteen degrees colder today. That should clear cobwebs from my head and the sunshine will do me good.

But honestly, the thought of changing out of my pajamas—long fleece pants and a T-shirt since Van doesn't even look at me if I'm dressed in skimpy clothes—has me reconsidering. Maybe I'll try to take a short nap before getting back to work, but I know as soon as I lie down and close my eyes, my brain will spin in constant rumination about my husband.

Indecisive, I stand in the kitchen, trying to decide what to do, but as fate would have it, someone knocks on the door, jolting me with surprise.

I look down at myself. I'm not even wearing a bra under the T-shirt, but it's Van's and swamps me. I'm wearing his clothes because that's the closest I can get to him and the smell brings me comfort.

Fuck it.

I pad through the living room, looking through the peephole before I open the door. I'm stunned when I take in the blond woman on the other side. I jerk back in shock but surely I'm mistaken.

She knocks on the door again and I bring my eye to the peephole for confirmation.

Yup… that's who I think it is.

Unlocking the dead bolt, I pull open the door and the woman smiles at me. "Simone… hi… I'm Brienne Norcross."

She offers her hand and I take it without hesitation for a brief shake. "Um… hi."

"May I come in?"

I snap out of my daze and scramble back, sweeping my arm for her to enter. "Of course. Come in."

Brienne Norcross is about as close to American royalty as you can get. As CEO of Norcross Holdings, she is a multibillionaire and also the owner of the Pittsburgh

Titans. I don't know exactly how old she is but I think early thirties, and she's exquisite with her blond hair in a sophisticated twist, flawless complexion and a ruby stain on her lips to match her red power suit.

As I close the door, she looks around at the interior of the house. I don't even know how Van came up with this place since he won't talk to me, but it's been renovated recently and it's quite beautiful. My gazes fall on my blanket and pillow and Brienne sees it too.

"Was watching TV last night on the couch," I explain as I move to fold the blanket.

"I always fall asleep with the TV on," she says. "Guess it's the only way to stop my brain from working. Drake hates it though so I have to wait for him to fall asleep and then I can turn it on. I'm definitely the night owl in our relationship."

I knew through the sporting news grapevine that Brienne was dating the Titans' goalie, Drake McGinn, but I see her sporting a massive diamond on her left finger, so I'm assuming they're engaged. I'm going to guess that's happened in the last few weeks as I haven't been watching much in the way of news. I've been too focused on my marital troubles.

"Um… can I offer you some coffee?" I ask.

"That would be lovely," she says and follows me into the kitchen.

I close my laptop, push it to the side and nod at the

table. "Please... sit."

Brienne is silent as I prepare her a cup of java and I'm relieved she takes it black since there's no cream or sugar in the house. Van drinks his coffee black and I can't have it, so there's been no need to have the necessary accompaniments. It's not like I'm doing any entertaining.

Sliding into the chair opposite Brienne, I can't help but ask, "Why are you here? I mean... you're clearly here to see me since Van's on an away trip, but how did you even know I was here?"

Brienne takes a delicate sip of the coffee and sets the cup down. "Your brother's worried about you. So he passed word on to Baden who came to see me."

I was aware my brother knew Baden Oulett, the Titans' goalie coach. Malik's company, Jameson Force Security, has done a customized security system for the home he and his fiancée Sophie renovated.

"And what exactly did my brother pass on to Baden, which got passed on to you?" I ask, not quite managing to keep a polite lilt in my voice. I'm pissed at Malik.

"That you're here alone. That Van left you to join the Titans and asked you for a divorce." I wince at her blunt words. "You followed him here to make it work but he's making it difficult. That you're lonely."

"Jesus," I mutter, pinching the bridge of my nose. I offer her an apologetic smile. "I am so sorry he laid that on your doorstep. He had no right and I'm perfectly fine."

"You don't look fine," she says with brutal honesty. "You've got dark circles under your eyes, which are also red and puffy. I'm guessing crying, not sleeping, or both."

I don't bother denying what she can so obviously see. "I appreciate your concern but you've got far more important things to manage than checking on me."

"I'm not here to check on you," Brienne says with a dismissive wave of her hand. "I'm here to help you."

I blink at her in confusion. "Pardon?"

"You're part of the Titans family, Simone. You need friendship and I've got a whole slew of ladies waiting to bring you into the fold."

"I'm not really part of the family," I mutter, sinking a bit in my chair. "Van has asked for a divorce and I followed him here uninvited. He doesn't want me at the games."

"Fuck him," Brienne says, and I actually gasp. "Your brother passed on to Baden who passed on to me the reasons why Van left you and wants the divorce. I also know that you think his reasons are bullshit and you're attempting to knock some sense into your husband. You are most certainly a part of this team and if Van doesn't like it, well then... I'm glad to release him from his contract."

My jaw sags, my mouth hanging open. I can only stare at her, completely in awe and slightly terrified of the power she wields.

"Please don't cut him from the team. This is the only joy he has right now."

"As long as he's not actively hurting you, which I will not abide, then his position is safe."

"He's not hurting me," I rush to assure her. I mean, he is, but it's through inaction. Still, I'm not going to jeopardize Van's career. "He's merely ignoring me and my attempts to talk to him."

"At least you're here... in the house. That has to account for something," she says hopefully.

"I forced my way in and refused to leave. He pretty much stays away... only coming in late at night to sleep."

Brienne's eyes cut to the couch. "I'm assuming not in the same room as you."

"Sadly, no," I grumble with frustration and I'm not sure why I'm suddenly at ease, but it all comes gushing out. "I've tried to seduce him to no avail which has always been the best way to get him to open up. I've tried harassing him and poking him and in all ways tried to annoy him because even anger is better than silence. I'm getting nothing. He's so caught up in this biography that came out and his insistence that it will ruin our—" I halt, not wanting to give away we were trying to have kids. "He's afraid that the stigma will be too much for me to bear."

"Surely he'll change his mind once it all settles down. This will be yesterday's news before too long."

I snort with derision. "That stupid book keeps hitting the *New York Times* bestseller list. It's not dying down."

Brienne's expression turns grim. "He is getting hit by reporters at the arena every single day. He seems to be holding up okay and the entire team's position is simply *no comment*, but I'm sure it's frustrating for him."

I nod. "Yeah… I get it. I really do. I mean, I read the book. It's awful and so many things are distorted or are flat-out lies. Van hasn't read it, thank God, but he knows how vile his father was. I'm sure he's imagined the worst and he'd be right about it. Still… none of it matters to me. None of it matters to the fans. That was proven when he was first outed as Arco's son three years ago."

"Why's he so upset now?" Brienne asks.

I can't tell her the real reason. That the stakes are higher with children involved. Instead, I lift a shoulder. "I think this is worse. Before it was just an article, but now it's an entire book built on Arco's personal diaries. It brings back a lot of horrible memories for Van."

Brienne drums her fingertips on the table, appraising me. "I'm sure he'll come around."

"I don't think he will." My voice cracks and I blink

back the tears threatening. I'm so fucking sick of crying. "I was actually thinking of heading back to Vermont."

Blinking in surprise, Brienne leans forward. "You can't give up. You haven't even been here a week."

"No offense," I say with resignation, "but I'm exhausted to the bone from trying. And besides that, it's hard to get my husband back when I can't even get near him. He's become a master at avoiding me."

"Well then," Brienne says, a sparkle of deviousness in her eyes, "we'll just have to find a way to put you in his path, won't we?"

I can't help but frown. "What do you mean?"

"I mean... you're coming to the games for starters. Special guest in my suite. That means you'll come to the after-parties."

"Van won't like that."

"And as you will be my guest, I'm betting he won't have anything to say about it." Brienne chuckles. "Also, did you know we have a family lounge at the arena? You can hang out there all day on game days if you want."

"He's going to be so mad," I muse, imagining Van's expression if he were to walk into the lounge on game day and find me there.

"Isn't that what you want? To provoke his emotion?" she inquires.

Yeah... that's exactly what I want. If I can at least have proximity to him, I can work my magic. I feel exhilarated all of a sudden, a well of hope surging within me. I'm back in the game and with Brienne at my back, Van's not going to be able to hide away from me completely.

A genuine smile splits my face. "I don't even know how to thank you."

"Invite me to the renewal of your vows or something," Brienne says with a laugh, pushing up out of her chair. "Now… go get a shower. Eat some food. Maybe take a nap. But tomorrow night, be ready. I'm putting together a girls' dinner to introduce you to some new friends that I think you desperately need. I'll have my driver come by and pick you up at seven p.m."

"But—"

"No *buts*, Simone." She walks to the door and opens it. Turning back to look at me, she repeats, "Be ready tomorrow night at seven. And the night after, I'll also have my driver pick you up for the game. That way you can drink and have fun."

"Um… I don't drink," I say. *Not with a baby on board.*

"No matter. You won't have to worry about driving, then."

"I don't know about dinner tomorrow night," I say fretfully. "I mean… Van will be coming back and I might get a chance to talk to him."

Brienne's mouth curves into a crafty smirk. "Or… he

could wonder where in the hell you are and it would eat him up."

Oh my God… she may be as devious as I am when it comes to wearing Van down. I grin at her. "Okay… I'm in for dinner and the game."

Then she's gone and I have to wonder if I imagined it all. But no, that was indeed Brienne Norcross breathing new life into my campaign to reclaim my husband.

And I'm here for it.

CHAPTER 7

Van

S KATING OFF THE ice for a line change, I drop onto the bench and accept a bottle of water from one of the trainers. I squirt it in my mouth and absently hand it back over my shoulder.

I follow the action with Coen leading the first line. He executes a crisp pass to Stone on the far side. Stone cradles the puck on his stick, his eyes scanning the ice for a perfect opportunity. He spies Boone darting toward the net, creating a distraction for the Dragon defense.

Stone whips the puck toward the net and I hear the Los Angeles crowd gasp at the speed with which it careens toward their goalie. Fate has a different plan for us as the Dragon goalie scoops it out of the air in an impressive display of athleticism that has the fans roaring with approval.

"Fuck," I growl. That was a good fucking play, executed flawlessly, only to be denied by a remarkable save.

Such is the nature of the game.

And admittedly, something I'm enjoying. The intensity of competition has been a bit of a balm to my soul. It lets me evade the horrors of my reality. When I feel the chill of the arena, the sound of blades cutting through ice, it transports me to an almost fantasy dimension where I can escape completely.

Coming back to pro hockey was the best decision I've made in a long time.

A minute and a half later, I'm back on the ice with my third-line mates. This is only our fourth game together and we've had only two practices, but we're meshing well. Our center, Anders Blom, is a young kid at only twenty-three, drafted from the Swedish Hockey League. He'd been down in the minors when the plane crash happened and was pulled up to join the new squad. He needs some seasoning and according to our GM it's one of the reasons they wanted me on the team.

Many came up from the minors and are young—at least by my standards at thirty-one.

Our left-winger, Evgeny Denisenko, is twenty-five but sometimes acts thirteen. I've quickly figured out he's the prankster on the team and the one always cutting up at practice. I don't say anything, though, because when he's on the ice with me in the heat of battle, he's fucking solid.

Dillon Martelle is the third-line right-winger and he's closer to my age than the others. At twenty-eight, he's married and has two kids. He spent most of his career in the minors but is playing super competitively this year.

Lastly, Mason Lavoie is my defense partner. A hulking kid of nearly six foot seven, he's only nineteen and one of the youngest on the team. He's whip-smart and fairly agile, despite his size. His biggest weakness I can see so far is his uncertainty about when to act the enforcer. His blood doesn't run hot the way mine does and I tend to push boundaries when out on the ice. Callum specifically wants him to learn from me, so we've had a few talks.

With every stride, every check, every calculated move, I immerse myself in the rhythm of the game. The familiar sounds of skates carving the ice, sticks clashing, and the thud of the puck hitting the boards are a symphony that guides me forward.

Yes, coming back to the league was the best thing for me. It's what I needed… to replace Simone. I immerse myself in the battle, letting my emotions ebb and flow as the momentum shifts back and forth between us and the Dragons. We trade goals, both sides refusing to back down. The tension in the arena is palpable as the clock winds down to the final minutes. Every shift counts—every play could be the difference.

In these crucial moments as the final seconds tick, I find solace in the camaraderie of my teammates. I'm the newest member of the Titans, but in the last six days, I've had nothing but their unwavering support. They've accepted me into the brotherhood with open arms and I've done my best to give it back. When I was with the Cold Fury, always hiding in fear that my true identity would be revealed, I kept myself closed off from everyone.

I'm not doing that this time.

While I might not be a fuzzy teddy bear, I'm forcing myself to develop relationships. This is my new family now.

♦

OFTEN, AN EAST Coast team would finish a West Coast game and fly back that night across the country. Tonight we're staying in LA though since we have two days until our next home game and we had a late-night flight yesterday. The team is exhausted and the powers that be who created the schedule budgeted a night's stay so we could sleep in real beds rather than in airplane seats.

It's evident we're close to the playoffs as normally many of the players would hit the bars in a place such as Los Angeles, especially after a win tonight. But every single one of them head up to their rooms, although a few stopped in the lobby bar for a beer.

I was invited but declined, wanting to give Etta a call before it got any later. She's in Redding and on West Coast time. She would have been at tonight's game except for a broken ankle that has her laid up.

Once in my room, I shed my suit, making sure to hang it up. Clad in only my briefs, I settle onto the bed with all the pillows propped behind me.

I dial Etta and she answers on the first ring. "Oh, Van… you played so good tonight. I was cheering you on so hard. Could you hear me?"

Laughing, I put her on speakerphone so I don't have to hold it up to my ear. "Yeah… I heard you."

"Ugh… I'm so disappointed I couldn't be there."

"How are you feeling?" I ask. Poor Etta missed a step on her back deck and rolled her ankle. Thank fuck Mark wasn't working that day and was there to help her.

"I'm fine. Still feeling stupid for not paying attention. But Mark's been taking very good care of me."

I have to admit, I wasn't happy when Etta started dating Mark Casperson. He's a veterinarian specializing in reptiles, which I thought surely would be a deal breaker for her. But no… turns out love is stronger than her fear of snakes.

Eventually, I got over it, mostly because it's what Etta deserves. She put her entire life on hold to take me in and raise me with love and devotion. I want her to have all the happiness in the world.

"Speaking of taking care of someone," Etta says, and my entire body locks because I know where she's going. "Where is that sweet wife of yours? I've put in a few calls and texts the last couple days and she's not answered. Is she out on a research trip?"

Etta doesn't know we've separated. I haven't had the guts to tell her because I know she'll land firmly on Team Simone. Etta read the book when it came out and while she doesn't discount my feelings about it she's managed to put it out of her mind, calling it "ridiculous clickbait." She has no clue how far it's caused me to spiral. How it's why I'm back in the league so I could run far away from my normal life with Simone.

"Van?" Etta says, bringing my attention back to her question.

"Um… I'm sure she's just busy," I say lamely, knowing that will spark more questions.

"What's going on?" she asks, in a tone that says I better not bullshit her.

I sigh and rub my hand along the back of my neck, digging into the muscles knotting with tension. "Simone and I are getting a divorce."

"Like hell you are," she snaps. "You two are the perfect couple."

"We're not," I say wearily.

There's a long, drawn-out silence but finally, she says, "Tell me everything."

"There's nothing to tell. I asked her for a divorce."

What follows is a litany of curses so loud, I have to turn the volume down on my phone. She ends by saying, "Now Van Turner… you owe me a lot and I've never once asked you to pay up for the way I rescued you, but I'm demanding you tell me the full story because in a million years you'll never convince me that Simone is on board with this."

"She's not," I admit without any pretense. "She's firmly against it."

"Is there someone else?" Etta asks, and I can hear in her voice that she's dreading the answer.

Yeah, Etta. His name is Arco and he's fucked up my life.

"No. It's not like that."

"Then what the hell is it like?" she demands.

I know that after I hang up with Etta, she's going to call Simone, no matter that it's nearly two a.m. on the East Coast. I know Simone won't lie to any direct questions. She loves Etta as much as I do.

I know I have to give her the full truth. "Simone and I have been trying to get pregnant."

"Oh," Etta gasps, and I can even imagine her putting her hand over her mouth, expression brimming with hope. "A baby."

"I can't do it," I say, the words tasting bitter on my tongue. "I can't bring a kid into my world, Etta. This book changed it all. It says horrible things about me and it provides even worse details about the crimes Arco committed. It's not fair to Simone and it would be bordering on abuse to make my kids suffer with that. You, out of anyone, know how bad it was for me. How cruel people can be when you have such a dark stigma attached to you. So I decided I didn't want kids, came back into the league and asked Simone for a divorce."

"No," she says. "No way. It didn't go down like that. You're leaving something out."

Jesus, I hate how perceptive she is. "Simone said she'd give up the idea of kids if it bothered me that much, but I can't do that to her. She was born to be a mother, and you know that. I'm giving her a divorce so she can have a happy life."

"Her happy life is with you," Etta retorts. "You don't have the right to tell her otherwise."

None of this is a surprise. It's why I'd been dreading talking to Etta about it. Like I said... one hundred percent Team Simone.

"I'm not going to argue with you about it," I say, the exhaustion over the topic clear in my tone. "This is my life, too, and I have a right to do what I think is best."

It kills me when I hear a tiny sob. Etta's voice is watery. "How can you cut out someone you love? How can you cut out the best thing that ever happened to you?"

"You're the best thing that ever happened to me," I say, but that's not exactly true. I'd say Etta and Simone are probably tied in that respect.

"Van... please don't do this to her. She's a beautiful soul and you're going to crush her."

My chest squeezes so painfully, it robs me of my breath. I can't even respond because the pain I'm causing Simone comes back on me tenfold. But, I do as I always do when my heart screams at me.

I remind myself that my children would feel the same way when they're being verbally tortured by other kids. Simone's just going to have to bear it along with me so we don't bring it down on precious souls too delicate to handle the cruelty.

"I'm sorry, Etta. But my mind is made up. I'm giving Simone the best chance at a strong marriage with children. I'm giving her the best chance at true happiness."

"You're an idiot," she snaps, and it's not lost on me that Simone has called me that once or twice in the last few weeks. "Where's Simone?" she demands.

"She followed me to Pittsburgh. I'm sure she hasn't called you back because she didn't want to be the one to break this news to you."

Another silence and I'm trying to think of something to say to make Etta feel better about this. But then she cuts my legs out from under me. "Twenty-three years, Van. That's how long you've been under my wing and I've loved you like no other. You've been everything I could hope for in a child and my pride knows no bounds where you're concerned. But tonight... you disappoint me. For the first time in twenty-three years, I'm ashamed of you."

And then she hangs up on me.

I'm so stunned, I just stare at my phone, so many emotions barreling into me that it takes a while to process what just happened.

Etta removed herself from my corner, a place she's lived for over two decades.

Now I'm truly alone.

CHAPTER 8

Simone

I'M LAUGHING SO hard my stomach hurts, and if I had a full bladder, I'd probably pee my pants. The other women around the table have heard this story before, but they're laughing just as hard.

I gasp, wiping tears away as I shake my head at Tillie. "I can't believe you did that to Coen's yard." She turned his deck and backyard into a veritable zoo by covering it with bird- and small rodent food, salt licks for deer and numerous gaudy birdhouses to attract feathered friends. It seems they were neighbors and there was a real enemies thing going on. "What did he do?"

Tillie snickers, running her finger over her wineglass. "Oh, he threatened me, bullied me and made me clean everything up. But... well, then..." She blushes, her smile turning soft and reminiscent. "Let's just say provoking Coen not only angers him but turns him on."

Pain lances through me at the potent reminder. That's exactly how it is with Van. Or at least, that's how it was when I first captured him.

Not so much these days.

"What about you and Van?" Harlow asks. "How long have you two been married?"

It took me a hot minute to get everyone's names down. Harlow's engaged to Stone and she's an attorney. Throughout dinner, I've learned a lot about these ladies that Brienne congregated, offering me a ready-made tribe of women to lean on.

"Two years," I say, lifting my water glass to take a sip. "Been together three."

"He's such a good addition to the team," Jenna says. She's engaged to one of the assistant coaches, Gage Heyward. "They could really use someone with his experience heading into the playoffs."

My eyes cut to Brienne and I've been wondering all night if she told anyone the truth about my marriage and how close it is to dying a horrible death. Only she and Sophie know since Malik opened his big dumb mouth. Oh, I gave him hell about it today in a phone call where I cursed him out, but then grudgingly admitted I was happy to be going for dinner with the women tonight.

The mere fact that I'm being asked questions about Van without any hint there's something wrong tells me both ladies haven't said a word. It doesn't feel quite right to let them believe that everything is okay.

"Um… actually, I think you need to know that we're separated."

They all look at me with shock and sympathy. It's Ava—Coach West's girlfriend—who grabs my hand. "Oh, I'm so sorry."

"But Van just got to the team last week," Danica says with concern. She's dating Camden. "It happened after you got here?"

I blow out a huge breath, looking around the table. "It's actually a little more involved than that. And separated isn't the right word. He left me in Vermont without even telling me he was coming back into the league."

"That asshole," Stevie says, and I like that she speaks her mind. I learned tonight that she owns a bar and is dating Hendrix.

"I agree," I say with a laugh, accepting the humor in her proclamation.

"It's because of the book," Kiera says, and my head swivels her way. "It's got him all twisted up and he's running from it."

My jaw sags open and I just gape at her. "How did you know?"

"I remember when that first article came out about his dad," Kiera says. She's deep in the hockey world as her brother is Drake McGinn, the same Drake engaged to Brienne. "Didn't y'all split up then?"

I nod. "Yeah. He flipped out when that happened and it caused a rift between us. But he fixed it."

"And here you are again, dealing with the emotional fallout from that bastard's book," Sophie grumbles.

Stevie raps her fist on the table, turning everyone's attention to her. She motions around the table. "I'm sort of new to this group, just like you, but I can tell you, no one will have your back like these women. Brienne brought you into the fold and now you have all of us. I get that you don't know us, but that will change very quickly as we've got a long dinner planned for tonight whereby we're going to divulge all to each other. But... just so you know... I'm the woman who you come to for revenge and retribution. I'm the one who will call Van the asshole and figure out ways to help destroy him if he can't get his head out of his ass. Also, I have access to several mean, burly bikers who will break knees for fun and not money. So there's that."

I stare at Stevie a moment before I burst out laughing, as do all the other ladies. Chatter wells as they tease her for being the ball-buster and my eyes find Brienne's. She's been mostly silent, letting the other ladies pull me into conversation, but her message is clear as she returns my look. *See... I told you. We've got your back.*

♦

MY SPIRIT IS light as I walk up the front porch of Van's house.

And immediately becomes heavy as I realize that

without any thought, I referred to it as *his* house and not *our* house. I glance over my shoulder at the limo pulling away from the curb. Along with it goes all the happy vibes that bolstered me throughout the night.

The house is dark inside, although the porch light is on. That's not Van's doing, as I had turned it on before I left for dinner. I know the team plane touched down hours before the limo arrived to pick me up, but Van hadn't come home at that point. He might be inside now or he might still be out... who knows. But I can guarantee if he's in there, he's already locked away in his bedroom so he doesn't have to deal with me.

I unlock the door and slip inside, quickly silencing the beeping alarm panel by punching in the four-digit code. I set my keys on the table, let my purse slip to the floor and turn to find a huge, hulking figure in the dark.

I shriek with fear but immediately, even in the shadows, recognize Van.

"Where the fuck were you?" he demands.

I reach back, flip on the living room light and take in his angry expression. It's the most emotion I've seen from him in days and it's five actual words he's said to me.

I'm almost giddy from the attention and I want more. I push past him. "Not sure it's any of your business, really."

Van's hand clamps on my upper arm and he pulls me

to him. "Your safety is my business," he growls low in his throat. "I was worried something happened to you because your car was here but you weren't. You could have left a goddamn note, Simone."

"Kind of like the way you let me know you were leaving on an away trip? You haven't said two words to me in days, Van. Why would I give you the courtesy?"

I know that sounds petty and in truth, I didn't think he'd even be here to worry about me, which is why I didn't leave a note, but I hope the point is made that it hurts being left in the dark.

"You still haven't told me where you were," he says.

I don't owe him anything, but I give him the truth. "I was out with friends."

"Malik and Anna?" he asks, hand still holding me tight.

I can't figure out if he's driven by jealousy or true concern but either would be fine with me. Something to make me believe he cares.

"Malik and Anna are family, not friends," I say.

"You don't have any friends in Pittsburgh." I can see the anger burning bright in his eyes, which means he's jealous. Ordinarily I'd use that as a weapon but one thing I'll never do is lead him to believe there would be someone else. "I went out with Brienne Norcross and some of the other Titans women. She sent a limo for me, so how could I decline?"

Van releases me so suddenly, I stumble back. "Brienne Norcross?" he asks aghast. "Why the hell would you be with her? Or the Titans women?"

I snap at him hotly. "Because they happen to care that I'm here in a foreign city by myself and that I'm lonely."

"And how did they know you're here and lonely?" he snarls, his face reddening with what I think might be embarrassment. "Did you call Brienne and let her know what a douche your husband was for leaving you behind? Did you cry out all of your misery to my fucking boss?"

"No, Van." My voice is quiet... calm. "Malik told Baden. Baden told Brienne. Your boss showed up on the doorstep and was intuitive enough to know something was wrong the minute she saw me. I think it was the dark circles under my eyes from lack of sleep or the fact they were red from constantly crying. Take your pick. But she had the decency to ask me what was wrong and I told her the truth."

Van's expression crumbles. "I'm sorry," he whispers. "You know I'm not trying to hurt you, right?"

It's the first moment of true vulnerability I've seen from him and I move quick to take advantage. I walk right into him, pressing my body against his muscular frame. My hands slip over his shoulders and I tip my head back. "You're hurting me all the same. You've shut me out and you're not giving me the chance to fight for you."

Van doesn't return my touch but he doesn't pull away either. His voice is gravelly. "I don't want you fighting for me. I want you to forget about me."

I shake my head adamantly. "Never. It won't happen. I'm not moving on from you, baby, and the sooner you accept that, the sooner we can start fixing things."

"I can't—"

I grab his hand and pull it to my chest, forcing his palm over my heart. "You're in here, Van. You're entwined with every cell in my being and to remove you would kill me."

His expression is a turbulent storm of angst, his jaw locked hard.

Words alone won't get him to soften all the way so I move his hand over my breast. My nipple puckers under the touch and Van inhales sharply before trying to pull away. I grip him hard. "Touch me, please."

His gaze drops to where his hand rests on my chest, indecision warring in his eyes. I want to reach out and touch him, but I think I'll die a million deaths if he's not hard. He always gets so hard for me with such little provocation.

Instead, I grab his other hand hanging loose at his side and force it between my legs. "Touch me here."

Van's hand reflexively squeezes and my hips jerk, a tiny moan escaping.

It's that tiny sound that seems to snap Van out of a daze and he wrenches away from me. I'm breathing hard, a mixture of desire and pure frustration. I can't help myself… my gaze drops down and I'm somewhat mollified by the thick line of his erection through his jeans.

"You still want me," I point out bluntly. "Why are you pulling away?"

"I'll want you to the day I die, Simone. But that doesn't change a damn thing."

"Aaagghhh," I scream with frustration, my fists balled up and I stomp my foot. "Why are you being such a pigheaded asshole? Why do I even love someone like you?"

Van's expression remains impassive and for the first time in one of our fights, he's not the first to turn away. I march toward the door and bend to pick up my purse. I swipe my keys from the table and jerk the door open.

"Where are you going?" Van asks.

I ignore him, stepping over the threshold and slamming the door behind me. I'm halfway down the steps when the door opens and he calls out again, "Simone… where are you going?"

I throw my middle finger up in the air. That should be answer enough.

"Simone," he barks but I head straight for my car, intent on putting as much distance between us as I can tonight.

The man is stealthy, I'll give him that. He catches up to me and takes me by the elbow, halting my progress. "Have you been drinking tonight? Because if you have, I'm taking your keys."

Funny how simple words slice deep. *No, I haven't been drinking because I'm pregnant with your child.*

"I haven't been drinking," I say calmly. "Now let go."

"Where are you going?" he asks again, although he releases me.

"Malik's." I don't offer more because I'm not sure that's where I'm really going. I just know I want away from Van right now.

He studies me for a moment but then nods. "Just be careful, okay?"

I struggle not to scoff. Instead, I turn away from him and walk around the front of my car. Van doesn't go back in the house but watches me with his hands tucked in his pockets. Normally, I'd give anything to know what's going on in that beautiful head of his but right now, I don't care.

When I pull away, I know immediately the thing that will make me feel better. It's not going to Malik's and it's not calling any of my family members.

I dial Etta.

She called me first thing this morning and I didn't

answer because I had been avoiding her. I wasn't sure what she knew and I figured it was up to Van to let her know what was going on. She left a voicemail, which included a few nasty but choice words about him and it became clear to me that she knew everything, so I called her right back.

We had a good talk. I had a good cry. She vowed to help me in any way she could. She was the first official member of my female tribe. Brienne and the others completed it tonight.

"Hi, honey," she coos when the line connects.

"I hate him," I snarl into the phone as I drive to God knows where. I don't know my way around at all, but it doesn't matter. I can use Google Maps to find my way back.

"You don't," she says softly. "You love him so much that you want to hate him."

"I can't reach him," I lament. "It would be so much easier if he didn't love me. If he didn't care. Why can't he be normal and just have an affair or something to break the marriage up? Why is he choosing the dumbest reason of all?"

"You know it's not dumb to him," she chastises. "As much as I disagree with what he's doing, he's in emotional overload. He's making what he thinks is the best decision to protect you."

He's more chivalrous than that, I think to myself. He's

doing it to protect the kids we'd planned on having. I don't tell Etta I'm pregnant. I can't trust her to keep that secret from Van. Only Anna knows and that's the way I'm keeping it.

"I'm out of ideas, Etta. I've tried to reason until I'm blue in the face. I've tried to seduce him. I've screamed at him. Cried. Nothing is getting through."

"Time," she says.

"What?"

"Time. It's going to take time for this to settle. This is going to fade away. You and I both know that and he'll see it won't follow him."

Bitterness weighs on me. "Until the next story comes out and he runs."

Etta doesn't deny that, but how can she? This is twice now Van's flaked out on me because of his dad. If I did repair things, could I trust it to stick?

I have no clue.

"I love you, honey," she says sweetly. "You know that, right?"

"Of course I do. I love you too."

"It's my deepest wish you two work this out. I believe you are soul mates. But you need to consider that Van might not have it in him. Because I love you, I want you to be happy and it might not be with him."

I'd ordinarily rail against such a notion, but I don't have the energy.

"However," she continues, "it is far too early to be throwing in the towel. I need you to shore up your resolve and go back at him swinging. You stay in his face and you continue to harass him. You make him understand, okay?"

I smile at the vehemence in her tone. It gives me a little strength. "Okay. I will."

"Do you want me to come?" she asks.

Yes. Because Etta is who Van respects most in the world. Her being here might change the tide. "No. I need to handle this. I can either make it work or it wasn't meant to be."

"I've got faith in you."

Those are nice words, but I don't believe them about myself. I think I'm just running on borrowed luck, and it feels like it's running out.

CHAPTER 9

Van

I FOLLOW BOONE through the parking lot of Mario's, nervous as fuck. It's my first time out in the public eye after a game and I have no clue if I'll get accosted by reporters. I'm still getting daily requests for interviews through the PR department and they show no signs of letting up. I guess they're not getting the hint that *no comment* truly means *no comment*.

It's the lesser of two evils, though—accepting my teammates' request to come out and celebrate with them or go home to Simone where we'll either fight or I'll break down and fuck her.

It almost happened last night. When she pressed her body into mine, it was sensory overload. My dick got so hard it was painful and then when she pushed my hand between her legs, my knees almost buckled. It took every bit of willpower to pull away from her, and I'm not sure I can do it again. I want her too much. I fucking jack off every day to the hundreds of memories I've built with her over the years and I'm resolved that's all I'll ever have.

"Van," a man calls out as we approach the door and I immediately tense. That's not the tone of someone who knows me personally but rather of someone who's trying to get my attention. There's most likely a camera poised, ready to take a picture, and I hunch my shoulders and keep walking behind Boone.

"Van," the man yells again and he sounds closer. Definitely a reporter judging by the eager inflection in his voice.

"Oh, fuck this," Boone snarls and whips around. I almost run into him, but he stomps past me and yells, "Don't you people have anything better to do? How many times do this team and Van have to say no comment?"

I turn to see that it is indeed a reporter and he's standing there with wide eyes, taken aback by Boone's attack. I clap my hand on his shoulder. "Come on, man. Let it go."

Boone grumbles in frustration but we pivot toward the doors to Mario's. On game nights they have extra security and when we enter, Boone points through the glass doors to the reporter still standing out there. "He doesn't get in."

The bouncer nods.

"No press gets in," Boone adds.

"Yes, sir."

I'm not sure Boone has the authority to tell them who can and can't come into an establishment, but it seems to have worked.

"Thanks for that," I say.

"Got your back." He then pushes past me, glancing over his shoulder as I follow him. "They've got a sectioned-off area back here for us." We wind through the crowd. "You can hang in there and keep a buffer between fans or mingle with them. They're usually super chill and respectful."

He says this to me because he knows I'm on edge about being in the media spotlight, not for being the newest addition to the Titans, but for being the son of a notorious serial killer.

"I'm good," I assure him. I've been practicing in my head what to say to the first person who asks about my dad or the book.

I would like to say "Fuck off," but pretty sure PR would frown on that. So instead, I'm going to be genial and just say, "We can talk about anything but that."

Some of the players and their significant others are already inside the area cordoned off with red velvet ropes. I ignore the sharp stab of guilt that Simone is banished to the house simply because I didn't invite her to the game, and the even sharper stab of longing to have her by my side. My line in the sand has been etched so deep it's a fucking chasm and I'm not going near it for fear of falling in and losing myself completely.

We step over the rope and come upon Hendrix and his girlfriend, Stevie, talking to Liam, Anders and Foster.

"Dude," Foster exclaims holding his fist out. "You made it."

"Figured it was time to hang out with you bozos," I drawl.

A waitress appears and I order a beer. Boone melts further into the crowd of players and their women, but I hang on the fringe. I'm more of an introvert and while I've become very at ease talking to my mates while on the ice, idle chitchat is still a bit uncomfortable.

I listen with half an ear as Anders complains about a bogus call that was made against him for hooking in the first period. It was indeed bullshit but he needs to let that stuff go. No sense in continuing to stress about it.

I should say that to him.

In a constructive way so that he understands I'm just trying to impart a dash of experience. That's one of the reasons Callum wanted me here, to bring some seasoning to the team.

I open my mouth to say just such a thing but something catches my attention behind him over near the bathrooms. My jaw drops to see Simone coming out of the ladies' restroom along with Baden's fiancée, Sophie, and Stone's girlfriend, Harlow. The three of them are laughing and even more shocking than seeing Simone here is the fact that she's wearing a Titans jersey with my name on it.

Christ, I can't even begin to process the emotions slamming around inside me. The first and ever-present is intense longing for the woman, not just because she's beautiful and sexy but because no one has ever loved me the way she has. I'm also perplexed that there's an animalistic pride in seeing her wear my jersey and I immediately banish that from my thoughts. She is not part of Team Van. She's not even supposed to be in Pittsburgh and I'm pissed as hell that she's here celebrating with my team because all that does is blur the lines for me.

She's not playing fair and I'm going to put a stop to it.

"Excuse me," I mutter and step across the ropes, heading toward Simone. It's Sophie who sees me first and nudges my wife to get her attention and then nods my way.

I plaster on a smile, lifting my chin to greet Sophie and Harlow before my attention cuts to Simone. I keep my tone pleasant, but to those who know me—my brat of a spouse, for instance—you can hear that I'm irritated. "Mind if I speak with you a moment?"

Sophie and Harlow exchange a look with Simone and I can see all I need to know about these women. They know Simone's side of the story and they know I'm not happy.

Harlow squeezes Simone's shoulder. "We'll meet you back at our table."

"Okay," Simone chirps with a smile. She watches them both melt into the crowd before turning to me. Her smile is pleasant, eyes sparkling as she hitches her purse higher on her shoulder, holding on to the strap with both hands. "You played a great game tonight."

I don't bother with niceties. "What are you doing here?"

Her look of confusion is overly exaggerated. "Why wouldn't I be here? My husband plays for the Titans. All the other wives and girlfriends are here."

Rubbing at my temple, which is now aching, I speak in low tones. "We're separated."

"We're living together," she points out.

"I've asked for a divorce and as such, you're not welcome at these events."

The smug look on Simone's face has me bracing for a slapdown. Her gaze cuts across the room and she waves at someone. I twist my neck to look over my shoulder and see Brienne and Drake standing there. Brienne blows a kiss back at Simone.

My wife turns her attention to me, cyes glittering with challenge. "I think Brienne would disagree with you on whether I'm welcome."

"Christ, you're a piece of work," I mutter angrily.

"Can I buy you a celebratory beer?" She looks so hopeful and I fucking hate to hurt her, yet again. But she's going to accept this and ignoring her is the best weapon I have.

"Pass," I say and turn on my heel. Not going to give her a minute of attention.

I can't even hope that by ignoring her she'll get frustrated and leave because she now has friends here. She'll hang out with her new cronies and have no incentive to leave. But at least she won't have my notice.

Before I reach the velvet ropes, a woman steps in my path. I'm brought up short, so lost in my thoughts I almost barrel over her.

It would be impossible not to notice she's beautiful but that thought only briefly crosses my mind. I'm more on guard wondering if she'll ask me about Arco.

"Van... hi... I'm sorry to stop you like this, but I wanted to tell you I'm a huge fan. I lived in Raleigh when you played for the Cold Fury and even had your jersey. My job recently transferred me here to Pittsburgh and I flipped out when I saw you joined the team. I just wanted to know if I could get a picture... I don't have anything to sign or else I'd be begging for an autograph too."

Some of the tension eases. "Yeah... sure."

She beams and flips the screen on her camera. She's got a beer in one hand and holds her phone out with the other for us to take a selfie. Her arm's not quite long enough to get us both in, so I take it from her. "Here… let me."

The woman scrunches in close but not inappropriately so. She smiles, I follow suit and snap a few photos.

As I'm handing her phone back, the waitress arrives with my beer. I start to fish out my wallet, but the woman says, "Oh, please… let me buy that for you."

She's got a twenty in her hand and the waitress makes change.

"Cheers," she says as she holds her bottle out and I tap the neck of mine against hers.

"Thanks." And now I feel obligated to talk to her.

I don't have a damn thing to say, feeling incredibly ill at ease given I'm an introvert and my wife is lurking somewhere. But she surprises me when she says, "How has it been coming into a zone defense when the Cold Fury played more man-to-man?"

I blink in surprise that she wants to talk hockey. And not because she's a woman but it's just most fans don't want to talk logistics.

I manage an actual smile—relief that this is just hockey talk—and don't feel out of place engaging. "Being out of the league for three years, it's all an adjustment. But I'm adapting."

"You most definitely are. I think this team is going to go far in the playoffs. Even has a real chance of going all the way."

"That's the dream, right?" I take a sip of my beer before asking, "So, are you now a Titans fan or still a Cold Fury fan?"

She grins. "You mean, who am I going to root for when they come here to play next week?"

"Time to pick a team…" My words trail off as I was going to insert her name.

She holds her hand out for me to shake and I don't hesitate. "Lauren."

"Pick a team, Lauren."

I note that she doesn't release her hold on me but instead, she steps in closer. "If you're open to it, I pick you. For tonight, anyway. Interested in getting out of here?"

Jesus fuck.

I try to slide my hand free, but she grips hard and steps in even closer, going up on her tiptoes to put her face closer to mine. "Sorry if this is overly forward but I wasn't kidding when I said you're my favorite player and I'd kill to have a night alone with you. I promise I've got no boundaries in the bed and you will walk away a happy man."

I'm on the cusp of jerking my hand free and taking a step back but then Lauren is suddenly ripped away from me. It takes me a split second to process that Simone has Lauren by the hair with one hand and the other has a fistful of the woman's sweater. She pulls her back so violently that Lauren's feet go out from under her, her bottle of beer flying.

"Holy shit," I bark and shove my beer at the person standing closest to me.

By the time my hands are free, Simone's on the floor with Lauren in a headlock and she looks like she's ready to commit murder. "I should kill you for touching my husband but as it stands, I'm just going to have a really good time stomping your ass."

"Get off me, you crazy bitch," Lauren screams and reaches back to grab a hunk of Simone's hair.

"Goddamn it, Simone," I yell, reaching down to break her hold on Lauren. "Let her go."

"Not until I get in a few good punches," she snaps back. "She said she has no boundaries in bed. Well, I've got no boundaries protecting what's mine."

She heard all that, huh? I hadn't even noticed her, but she must have been standing right behind me for that part.

Next thing I know, Boone is there and he's reaching down to help me untangle the women. He tries to pull Lauren free as I clamp onto both of Simone's wrists, but her hands are curled into tight claws in the poor woman's hair and clothing. "Let her go."

"Not until I teach her a lesson," she snarls.

"Oh, for fuck's sake, Simone. You're causing a scene."

I hate to say it and I'll never admit it, but my wife looks fucking fabulous. Her eyes are blazing and her skin is flushed, chest heaving as she wants to kill this woman for propositioning me. I get it because I'd feel the same if a man did that to Simone.

"Let go of her hair," I bark.

"Let me yank some of it out and I will," she throws back.

"Get this bitch off me," Lauren shrieks.

I can't hurt my wife, but she's got to release the other woman. I let go of one wrist and immediately put my fingertips to her ribs where I do nothing more than tickle her.

It's Simone's Kryptonite. She cannot stand to have her ribs touched, and she screeches the minute I start wiggling them against her.

Lauren is freed and Boone pulls her away from us. I latch onto Simone's upper arm, hauling her up and grabbing her purse off the floor. I start moving her through the crowd. She doesn't hesitate to let me guide the way until she sees the exit door looming and tries to put on the brakes.

"I'm not leaving."

"Yes, you are," I reply, pushing her along with ease.

When we reach outside, she tries to jerk away from me. "You can't just throw me out of here."

"I'm not throwing you out. I'm taking you home."

"But I don't want to go home. I was having fun hanging out with my girls."

"Yeah, well, that was a shit show of embarrassment. I doubt they'll want you back again."

I expected that to piss her off but instead, she falls silent.

"Where's your car?" I ask, still refusing to give up my hold on her. Not sure I trust her not to bolt across the parking lot to head back inside.

"Over there," she says with a nod.

"Give me the keys."

Without a fight, she reaches into her cross-body bag and hands them over. I unlock the doors remotely and escort her to the passenger side. She slides in sullenly and offers me a glare as I close the door.

She doesn't say a word to me as we drive to my house and just as we're pulling into a parallel spot out front, her phone rings. She nabs it from her purse and connects the call. Has to be one of her newfound female hockey friends. Her end of the conversation has my teeth grinding.

"Hey," she says softly into the phone with a brief pause before she says, "I'm fine." Another pause. "I'm positive. I'm good. He's making me go home."

I shoot her a glare but she's got her focus out the passenger window.

"I know. I'm sorry. I was really looking forward to hanging out with you tonight."

Guilt smacks me hard in the face and that pisses me off. I have nothing to feel guilty about. Simone made an ass of herself and the best thing was to remove her from the scene.

To be honest... I wanted to leave too. I didn't feel comfortable with her being there, not because I had intended to talk or flirt with other women. But I didn't like it that I'd told my teammates we were separated and divorcing and there she was, acting like we were together.

Sort of.

So fucking confusing.

We exit the car and I lock it, following Simone up the steps as she continues her conversation. "I didn't mean to lose my shit like that." Pause... listens to whoever is on the other end, and then she chuckles as I unlock the door. "You'd do the same thing, so don't pretend otherwise."

Jesus... how well does she know these ladies? She's only been friends with them for like a whole day. What in the hell did they talk about last night?

Simone sighs as I toss the keys on the table. I normally would head straight to my bedroom and lock myself away, but I'm far too curious to hear the rest of this conversation.

Walking into the kitchen, Simone opens the fridge

and pulls out a bottle of water. She holds her phone between her shoulder and ear as she listens to the other woman.

The minx has the nerve to shoot me a disapproving glare. I scowl right back, leaning against the counter and crossing my arms over my chest. I make no pretense that I'm doing anything but eavesdropping.

Simone paces back and forth, quietly listening before snorting at whatever's said to her. "I'm thinking it's not such a good idea for me to go to team events where Van might be looking to hook up with another woman. I can't handle it."

"I wasn't looking to hook up with anyone," I snarl as I push off the counter, pissed she's maligning my character to one of my teammates' significant others.

"Didn't look that way to me," she shoots back. "It was embarrassing the way you were flirting with her."

"Embarrassing?" I exclaim, advancing on her. "I'm not the one who assaulted another person tonight."

"It's your fault that I was in that position," she yells, then seems to remember someone's on the other line as her voice lowers. "I'm so sorry, Brienne. I need to disconnect now and have a serious conversation with my husband."

Jesus Christ… that was my boss checking in on my wife, worried that I had—what? Hurt her?

Simone disconnects, setting her phone on the table,

and I let her have it. "I cannot believe you'd fucking talk about our personal shit with Brienne Norcross. Are you trying to get me fired?"

"Well, what was she supposed to do when you man-handled me out of Mario's? She was concerned about me since I'm a hockey wife."

"You aren't a hockey wife," I bark at her.

"I'm well aware of that," she screams, and it's not her normal raised voice that's suffused with anger and frustration. It's filled with pain.

She spins away and lunges at her purse she'd set on the kitchen chair. Opening it, she pulls out a T-shirt and whirls to face me. Holding it up, she said, "They gave me a T-shirt tonight." She points to the pocket. "It says 'Titan Queens.'" She flips it around and I see on the back it says 'The real power behind the Titans.' My chest constricts over the kindness and cramps even further over the cruelty.

She balls it in her fist and shakes it at me. "But I can't wear it. I'm well aware that I don't have the right because you took that away from me. You took every-thing away from me."

Simone looks down at the shirt, as if surprised to see it in her hand. Then her face screws up in disgust and she marches over to the utility drawer, pulling it open. Out comes a huge butcher knife and she jabs it through the wadded-up cotton shirt and starts sawing at the material. It makes a decent-sized hole. She abandons the knife and uses her hands to rip it all the way to the seams.

She whips it at me, catching me in the chest, and my hands automatically snag it before it drops to the floor.

"Are you happy now?" she cries.

No, I'm not happy. I'm devastated for her right now. She may have done the act of destroying that shirt, but I'm the one who ruined all it stood for.

But maybe… just maybe… Simone will finally give up. Maybe this is the straw that will break her stubborn back and she'll go home to Vermont. I ignore my soul rebelling at the idea of her moving on, falling in love again, having a family.

It's what's best for her.

Simone just stands there staring at me, her chest rising and falling in agitation. I clutch the ruined shirt, afraid to say a damn thing.

I wait for her to come to the conclusion… it's best that she move along.

Except, it's not defeat I see dulling her hazel eyes. Instead, they're cold and calculating. They narrow in on me as if she's puzzling out a mystery.

Mustering up my most dispassionate, disconnected expression, I wait her out.

"Will you have sex with me tonight?" she asks, and the question is so random and not at all in context with the fight we just had that my jaw drops. I can't formulate words to answer her.

"No, huh?" Simone pivots on her foot, grabs her purse and phone. "Okay, then… I'm out of here."

There's something about the set to her spine and the way her shoulders are tossed back that makes me uneasy. "Where are you going?"

"Out." But she doesn't walk out the door, instead cutting up the stairs to the bedroom where she keeps her luggage. She's still sleeping on the couch to annoy me.

"Out where?" I ask, starting after her. By the tone of her voice, it seems incumbent upon me to find out more.

"Out to get laid," she says as she disappears into the bedroom.

"Like hell you are," I bark, taking the stairs two at a time. When I round the corner and enter the bedroom, I see she's digging through her suitcase. She's tossed her purse and phone on the dresser.

Holding up a minuscule black dress to observe, she nods her satisfaction and tosses the dress on the bed.

"You are not going out to get laid," I snap with irritation.

She ignores me and instead kicks off her boots and shimmies out of her jeans. She spares me a glance before pulling her sweater over her head.

When she reaches for the dress, she says, "You don't tell me what I can or can't do, Van. You want the divorce. You're the one pushing me away. You're the one who refuses to touch me. So fine. I'm going to go find someone who will rock my world tonight and then just maybe I can find the strength to leave you."

Fury such as I've never experienced sweeps through me, so intense and overwhelming, my vision dims. My hand flies out, wrapping around the front of Simone's neck and I walk her backward until she bangs into the wall. I place my other palm beside her head and bend down so my face hovers right before hers.

I make sure she's got her eyes locked onto mine so she has no doubt about my next words. "Until such time as we're divorced, you will not touch another man. You're certainly not going to do it just to punish me."

To punctuate that proclamation, I tear the dress free from her grip and toss it away.

"You don't own me," she whispers. "I can do whatever I want."

"No, baby," I murmur with a slight shake of my head. "You can't. I'll tie you to the damn bed if I have to."

The corners of her mouth curve upward, and I see a flash of triumph across her face. I can barely comprehend that look... that she feels like she's won something... then her hand is pressing against my crotch.

And there she finds me fully hard and I'm not even sure when that happened. I mean... I'm always on the verge of getting a hard-on around her. It's been that way for three years I'm so fucking attracted to her.

She squeezes me and I can't stop the groan that rips free.

"You know what you need to do, then," she taunts, running her palm up and down my cock now straining to bust free of my zipper.

Yeah… I know what I need to do.

And I hate myself for it.

CHAPTER 10

Van

MY HIPS PUNCH forward, a natural reaction to the grip Simone has on me. I drop my forehead to rest against hers, exhaling in defeat. I can't make myself pull away.

It's not that I'm afraid Simone will give herself to someone else because I don't believe her taunts for a minute. It's purely that I don't want to hurt her anymore tonight. I want to give her something because I've caused her so much pain and I know my touch and my attention will be a balm to her.

I also know it will confuse things, but she's pushed me past my breaking point.

"You want me to fuck you?" I ask, my voice hoarse with desire as she continues to stroke me.

Simone is oddly silent, so I lift my head to peer down at her. She nods while running her tongue over her lower lip. It takes all my willpower not to bite her.

Sliding my hand from the front of her throat to cup her around the back of her neck, I make sure she's clear on what this means. "You know it won't change anything. I'll make you come and still walk away."

Fire flashes in her eyes. Utter defiance and a slight smirk that tells me she believes she still has power over me. I can practically read her thoughts. *Yeah, baby... I remember. I remember you tried to do that three years ago when I was gunning hard for you and you always came back.*

"Just shut up and kiss me," she demands.

I stare at her hard, trying to find something within her expression that will turn me off this course, but another hard stroke on my dick distracts me.

Fuck it.

I pull her up to my mouth by the grip I have on the back of her neck and Christ... her lips against mine feel even better than her hands on my dick. Not sure how that's possible, but I have no intention of fucking my wife tonight so my dick doesn't matter.

Simone purrs into my mouth, greedy for the attention. Her tongue tangles with mine, and I lean into her, pinning her to the wall. It also traps her hand against my cock so she can't move it. I don't want to get sidetracked.

Inching my hand up the back of her neck, I grab a hunk of her hair and pull her head to the side. Trailing my lips down her neck, I'm satisfied by her full-body shiver. Love how much the tiniest touch affects her.

Simone has never been a docile participant and she

attempts to shove me back so she can stroke my erection. I sink my teeth into that tender area where the bottom of her neck slopes into her shoulder and she groans.

I reach down, grab her wrists and pull her hands away from me. I pin them to the wall.

"Let me go," she demands. "Let me touch you."

"Unless you want me to walk out of here, try to be obedient and keep your hands to yourself."

"But—"

"Let's not talk either," I add.

Simone glares at me but remains silent.

"Good girl," I praise, and I'm assaulted with what seems like a million memories of me ordering Simone to do something and her obeying beautifully.

She's always been my good girl.

Tentatively, I release her wrists and pause a moment as our gazes remain coiled up with each other. Then I'm jerking her bra down, relishing the way she gasps at the sudden move. I cover her breasts with my palms, squeezing their fullness and then pinching each nipple. Simone's hips jerk forward and then she sinks back against the wall. I let my eyes roam all over her, my emotions churning like a poisonous potion of lust and fury and self-loathing and love.

I want to fuck her so bad, but I won't.

But I will make her feel good, at least for the moment.

"Do you want me to make you come, baby?"

Her lips stay sealed but she nods.

I should splay her out on the bed, but why bother? Right here is good enough and not for the first time in my relationship with my wife, I sink onto my knees before her. A move I've done a hundred times, I peel her panties down her legs and she steps out of them gracefully.

Her body is a work of art and there's not a place on it I haven't explored thoroughly with my mouth, my fingers and a good deal of toys I've bought her over the years.

With a hand on the back of one thigh, I lift her leg high and drape it over my shoulder. Simone stares down at me with flushed cheeks, her palms pressed against the wall for balance. I drag my thumb down through the lips of her sex, find her soaking wet.

"Van," she wheezes.

My head snaps up and my hands fall away. "No words. Make all the sounds you want, but no words."

She nods frantically, biting down hard on her lower lip.

"This is for you, baby. It doesn't mean anything other than I want you to feel good right now."

Anger flashes in her beautiful eyes, but she keeps her mouth shut. I reward her by circling my thumb over her clit. "That's my girl."

Air gushes out of her and I don't waste any more time with teasing. I place a gentle kiss on her lower belly before running my tongue up her slit. Simone groans and I hear a thump, most likely her head falling back against the wall. I don't bother looking up because I am focused on making my love come.

I lick her just the way I know she craves, plunging two fingers inside her heat. Hungrily exploring every fold and crevice of her pussy, I savor the sweetness of my wife and her keening sounds of need echo in my ears. I show her no mercy, but she'd never ask me for it. I told her I wouldn't fuck her, but that's apparently a lie because I ruthlessly plunge my tongue and fingers into her tight channel. My dick is so hard it hurts, but I let that pain fuel my desire to give Simone the pleasure she deserves.

I wince as she takes fistfuls of my hair, gripping tightly. Her hips rotate against my mouth, silently demanding more. It brings back beautiful memories of the first time I went down on my wife. I can remember it as if it were yesterday, and I'm transported back in time because I'm going through the same exact thing with her.

After we first met, Simone pursued me relentlessly. She flirted, teased and taunted. The sexiest goddamn woman I'd ever known and she was hacking away at all my defenses. Chipped and chipped and chipped until I lost my shit.

I kissed her and it was everything I feared it would be. Sizzling hot and full of so much promise that she'd rock my world, I almost bolted.

Almost.

Instead, I tried my best to scare her off. "Get your ass in my bed and get naked. I'm going to show you what happens when you aren't smart enough to stop provoking me."

My words had the opposite effect, and it was excitement and triumph written all over her beautiful face.

Goddamn fucking, incorrigible brat.

That was my exact thought and it's what I think now. Here I am again, falling prey to her stubborn insistence that we belong together. Fuck if I don't love her more for her fierce determination.

I purse my lips on her clit, suck gently and then lash my tongue. Simone keeps her mouth shut but I can hear the moans deep in her throat. She holds my head in her hands, wantonly gyrating against my face, demanding more and more from me.

That first time I fucked her, it was done without any thought or care about how she felt. She dared me to do it and I put her right on her hands and knees and took her from behind. Best fucking pussy I'd ever had, and I had all intentions of busting a quick nut and walking away from her.

Except from the moment I drove inside of her, I knew that was just a pipe dream. Simone loved it hard and rough and didn't care that I wasn't whispering sweet nothings in her ear. She threw herself backward onto my cock, creating as much friction and pounding as I was trying to give her.

She was an animal and there was no way I could have ever stopped.

It was, up until that point in my life, the hardest orgasm I'd ever had. I shot my soul into her and when my heart rate came back down, I hated myself for my weakness. I flopped onto the bed, rolling to my back and staring at the ceiling with complete disgruntlement.

How in the fuck had she managed to do that to me?

Yeah… a goddamn fucking, incorrigible brat.

She wasn't finished with me, though. The scheming minx wanted more and wasn't giving me the chance to walk away from her. Simone rolled on top of me and fused her mouth to mine. I had no idea how much I needed that kiss, but I was immediately lost to it. And despite the fact I outweighed her by a good hundred pounds, she somehow managed to roll us so she was on her back and I was on top of her.

She fisted my hair, gave it a hard yank and then put a palm to the top of my head.

Eyes gleaming with lust and challenge, she pushed me down her body. She never said a word, but her intent was transparent.

What she needed was clear.

That fucking woman pushed me right down until my face was over her pussy. She spread her legs wide, tilted her hips up, and said, "Give it to me, Van."

And fucking Christ... I buried my face between her legs and gave it to her hard.

Just like I'm doing now.

Exactly like I did then.

It's come full circle for us, right in this moment.

Simone starts panting as I fuck her with my mouth and fingers, rotating her hips to maximize her pleasure. Taking alongside my giving. It's one of the things I love most about her... that she's not ashamed to ask for what she wants in the bedroom.

I've always, always given it to her.

With pure joy on my part.

Just like I am now.

I twirl my tongue around her swollen clit before battering it. I thrust my fingers in and out, and I have one small regret not being on that bed as I'd have one in her ass too.

Simone sucks air deep into her lungs, her fingernails scraping my scalp, and her hips buck hard as she starts to come. It came on fast and I wasn't prepared for it. I grip her ass with both hands to hold her still and suck on her clit hard to extend the orgasm. She shudders, gasps, pulls at my hair, but she never begs me to stop.

I'm the one who finally pulls away, turning my cheek to rest against her belly for only a second before I rise from the floor. I lick my lower lip, relishing her taste and already missing her body. My dick strains against my pants, my balls ache and my heart feels shredded. But at this moment, Simone is blissed out and I use the opportunity to put everything between us aside and enjoy the peace in her smile.

It lasts only a few moments before the haze clears and her expression turns wary.

She starts to move toward me, gaze cutting down to my erection. "Let me…"

I hold up a hand, take a step back. "Nothing has changed."

Simone huffs in irritation.

"I told you I'd make you come and then walk away."

"Yeah," she mutters, bending down to swipe her panties from the floor. She steps one foot in, then the other, shimmying them up her legs. "But I didn't think it would stop at just *me* having an orgasm."

I'm in the danger zone right now. My mouth wants to curve into an amused smile and I know the minute I fall prey to Simone's charms, she's going to have me giving up all that I believe in right now.

"Oh, I'm going to have an orgasm," I say, putting enough chill in my tone that the light in her eyes dies just a little. "Just not with you."

The words are meant to hurt and put distance between us… reminiscent of that first time we had sex and then she demanded I eat her pussy. I walked away after the orgasm faded, except I told her, *"Now that you're wearing my sweat on your skin, you've sort of lost your shine. Time to move on."*

Simone's shoulders slump slightly, the only indication that what I just said hit the mark.

I leave the room, not looking back. I trot down the stairs, straight into my bedroom where I lock the door behind me.

Within moments I have the shower on, the water hot, my body naked and my cock in my fist. Leaning my forearm against the tiled wall with the steam rising all around me, I bow my head and jerk off to the memory of what I just did to Simone.

CHAPTER 11

Simone

A RECEPTIONIST SITS inside the lobby of the arena's executive suite. It's only the second time I've been to the facility, the first being the game day before yesterday. Brienne had directed me to where I'd catch an elevator up to the top floor where double wooden doors lead into the inner sanctum of the higher-ups who run this organization.

A pretty young blond looks up from surfing her phone. Her desk is immaculate and there's no computer. I wonder if her only purpose is to greet people or answer the phone. She smiles brightly. "You must be Simone Turner. Ms. Norcross told me you'd be coming in to see her for lunch."

I'm surprised she knows that, given she has no apparent appointment calendar on her spotless desk, but I nod. "Yes, that's right."

"Follow me," she chirps as she stands.

I'm treated to a short tour as she points out various offices and conference rooms. We happen to walk by one office where I see Jenna at a desk, talking on the phone. She's a media liaison for the team.

Jenna sees me and waves with a bright smile. I wave back and continue, following the receptionist to a corner office.

The brass nameplate says Adam Norcross and I assume this must have been Brienne's brother's office. He died in the crash and she took over the team. I bet it's still hanging not because she hasn't had time to change it out but because she has no intention of doing so. It's an honorable nod to him and the work he did for the team.

The door is open and Brienne looks up to smile at me. The receptionist disappears and I'm motioned in as Brienne stands. "I'm so glad you could come over this way to have lunch with me."

She moves from behind the desk and walks straight to me for a hug. "Thanks for making time," I say as we pull apart.

"Come sit over here." She motions to a table that seats four in the corner. It has two place settings with a platter of roasted chicken and vegetables along with a fruit tray. "I had this brought in. Hope it's okay."

"Looks incredible." I look around the space as I move toward the table. "And your office is stunning."

"It's all Adam's style," she says as she plops down in a chair and immediately reaches for tongs to load up her plate. "I couldn't bear to change it."

It's clearly a man's office... pure masculine elegance with the Ohio River and the city skyline beyond the floor-to-ceiling windows. It's all dark woods and thick burgundy carpeting, heavy oil paintings in gilded frames.

Brienne hands me the tongs and I grab a chicken breast with roasted zucchini. I'm normally a healthy eater, but I suppose it's more important now that I'm pregnant.

There's a bottle of sparkling water along with a pitcher of iced tea. Brienne asks, "Which do you prefer?"

"The sparkling is great," I say and watch as she pours us each a glass.

I have to say... I like that. Brienne could easily have had a waiter here serving our food and beverages but she's such a grounded person, I can tell she's one of those who would rather do it herself.

I take a moment to cut up all my chicken and vege-tables while we talk about the game tonight. The team is in Atlanta playing the Sting but they'll head back after.

"Do you go to many away games?" I ask.

She smiles as she plucks a green bean from her plate with her fingers. "Not so many since Drake and the boys moved in. I'm hanging back with them." Smiling at me gently, she takes a bite of the veggie and points it at me while she chews. "I assume you're not at the point where you can attend some of the away games."

I shake my head, feeling glum about that observation. "No. Things aren't going well and after the debacle the other night at Mario's, Van would prefer I not come to any more games or events."

"Oh, bullshit," she snaps.

"Actually, I don't know that he's wrong." I set my utensils down. "It's why I wanted to come talk to you. I wanted to apologize for the way I acted at Mario's. I made an ass of myself and I hope I didn't embarrass you or the team. I know Van is horrified, but I wanted to assure you he's a true professional. I don't want my behavior to reflect poorly on him."

Brienne drops the rest of the green bean on her plate and uses a linen napkin to wipe her fingers. Her stare is empathetic, but there's an unyielding quality to her expression. "While I would prefer my hockey family not attack fans, it was defused quickly, thanks to your husband's quick intervention. I'm not worried about what happened. I did want to make sure you were okay, though, not because I thought Van would hurt you. It's clear he loves you a lot by just how idiotic this quest is for him to protect you from the history of his father. I wanted to make sure you were okay emotionally."

I snort. "Not sure I'm ever going to be better emotionally. Van is testing my limits."

"You're not wearing him down yet?" she asks.

I consider how I provoked him into giving me an orgasm the other night, so assured that if we could at least connect physically, it would bridge the emotional.

I was wrong.

I shake my head. "He's a stubborn man."

"Give it time," Brienne says. "You have a good history together and once some space can get between him and the book, he'll start to come around."

"Maybe," I hedge, but I'm not so sure. My confidence is at an all-time low.

Brienne's gaze hardens. "Regardless, you are a member of this hockey family and I don't care if Van doesn't like it, you are welcome at any games and events."

Laughing, I nod. "Okay… I'll make sure he knows that, but I think I'll pick and choose my battles."

"I assume you'll be here for the Cold Fury game at least."

"Yeah, wouldn't miss that for the world," I assure her. My brothers are going to stay after the game rather than fly back with the team for a long-overdue Fournier get-together. "I'll even be wearing a Titans jersey."

"Van's jersey," she corrects. "Or you could wear your Titan Queens T-shirt."

My face flushes. "Yeah… about that… it sort of got destroyed."

Brienne's eyebrows shoot high.

"I cut it up in a fit of rage during an argument with Van. I'm sorry."

Chuckling, Brienne waves off my apology. "I'll have

Jenna get you another one, and if that one gets cut up, we'll get you another. The point is, don't give up."

I manage a smile and stab a piece of chicken. I've been trying so hard, but I'm not gaining any ground. There will come a time when I'll give up.

The rest of lunch is pleasant and I learn more about Brienne personally, including more details of her clandestine affair with Drake, which turned into a beautiful engagement. We only chat for about thirty minutes, then Brienne is rushing off to a meeting.

I poke my head into Jenna's office to say hello, but it's empty. I grab a notepad and pen, jotting her a quick message to call me so we can get together. Van might not want me here, but I've already joined an amazing community of women and I'm going to take advantage of my time with them.

On the way back to the house, I make mental notes of how my week will progress. Van comes home tonight and with two home games ahead of us, there will be opportunities to interact with him.

Presuming he comes home.

The man won't sit down and have a rational conversation with me and everything devolves into a fight. I've fallen back on a tried-and-true method with Van, which is to provoke him into interaction with me, but that's not been working out so far. Sure, he broke the other night, but I know my husband well. Part of that was his regret for hurting and shutting me out. He was trying to give me something, even though he made things all the more confusing.

As I coast to a stop at a red light, I become aware that I have no clue where I am. I'd been so mired in my thoughts that I must've missed a turn somewhere and I'm in a part of the North Shore area I don't recognize.

"Shit," I mutter, immediately reaching for my phone that's connected to the navigation system. I flip to Google Maps and try to type in our address so I can get directions.

A car honks behind me and I see the light is green. I give a wave over my head in apology and hit the gas. As I drive, I try to type in the address with just my thumb. I also scan the neighborhood to see if I recognize any buildings.

I finally get the address in, hit Start on the directions and toss my phone on the passenger seat. I look up and see there's a red light right above me and I'm already halfway through the intersection.

Movement from my left catches my eye and I turn to see a large truck bearing down on me. A man is driving, his eyes wide open in shock to see me in the middle of the intersection while he has the right of way. He slams on his brakes and horn and it's all squealing tires until the front of his truck slams into my driver's side door. There's a horrific sound of tearing metal and my window explodes, raining chunks of tempered glass all around me. My car slides to the right a good ten feet and then both vehicles come to a rest, locked together.

My heart slams inside my chest and I'm dizzy from the shock of what just happened. I immediately do a systems check and realize I'm okay. Nothing hurts too terribly except for my left arm and hip, which took a blow from the door caving in, but definitely nothing broken.

Steam billows from the truck's grill and since my window is gone, it's wafting in front of my face. I'm able to get my seat belt off and then someone is opening my passenger door.

"Are you okay?" It's the man who was driving the truck.

"Yeah… I think so." I offer him a sincere apology. "I'm so very sorry. I was lost and wasn't paying attention. Totally my fault."

Luckily, the guy is more relieved I'm not dead than pissed and he helps me crawl over the console and out the passenger door. The police arrive quickly along with an ambulance. Statements are taken and insurance is exchanged. I'm issued a ticket and tow trucks come as neither vehicle is drivable.

An emergency medical technician checks me out and while my blood pressure is a little high and my arm is starting to throb, I don't think I need to see a doctor and

I tell him so.

"Are you sure?" he asks as he puts the blood pressure cuff away. "You took a pretty hard hit. You're going to be far sorer tomorrow than you are today."

"I can just take some ibuprofen or something…" My words trail off as I realize, I don't know if I can take any pain medicine without harming the baby. I don't know anything at all as I haven't had my first obstetrics appointment because I'm bound and determined to have my husband at my side. "Actually… I'm pregnant. Maybe I should get checked out."

"That's a good idea," he says with a smile on his face.

I don't want to ride in the ambulance but I sort of have to, given my car isn't drivable and the EMT guilts me into it because I'm pregnant. They make a concession, though, and let me sit in the "captain's chair" rather than on the gurney. I've never been in an ambulance before and I had no idea there was a chair a patient could sit in, but I gladly take it.

On the way, I call Anna and tell her about the accident. She makes arrangements for her mother to take Avery and assures me she'll meet me at the hospital.

"Don't tell Malik," I say before she hangs up.

"I won't," she assures me. "Not as long as things are okay."

"I'm fine. Just a precaution to get a checkup because of the baby and obviously, I'll need a ride home."

"All right... hang tight and I'll be there soon."

When we get to the hospital, I'm triaged quickly, given that I'm pregnant, and put into a curtained room. The nurse hands me a gown and instructs me to change into it, which I do, then I sit in one of the two chairs rather than on the bed. I'm determined to make this seem not as serious as it could potentially be.

When the nurse comes back in, she's pushing a rolling piece of equipment. "The doctor is going to need to do an ultrasound," she explains.

"No, he can't."

She blinks at me in surprise.

"I mean... I want my husband with me for the first ultrasound."

The nurse glances at her watch. "Well, it will be a little bit before someone from obstetrics can get here. How soon can he get to the hospital?"

I shake my head, tears coming hot and fast. "He's out of town." And he doesn't want me to be pregnant, so that's a bit of a sticking point.

The nurse places her hand on my arm. "I'm sorry, honey. You really need to have it done."

I nod, wiping at the tears. "Yeah... I understand."

"Is there someone who can be here with you?" She reaches over to a box of medical-grade tissues and pulls several out to hand to me.

"My sister-in-law is on her way." I dab at the tears.

"What exactly will I see on this ultrasound?"

"Given that you're only approximately seven to eight weeks along, not much. But the biggest thing we'll want to do is confirm a heartbeat."

"Okay," I say, gusting out a sigh of disappointment. I'm going to lose that first moment when we hear our baby together.

For a brief flash, I consider calling Van. He'd be at the visiting arena, doing pregame prep. I could tell him I'm pregnant, I was in an accident and that I'm scared. I could have him on FaceTime with me while we did the ultrasound.

Just as quickly, I discard that idea. It would mess up his game. It would mess him up... I mean, major fucking with his head and I can't do that.

Besides, I'm never going to lure him back with the baby. I know he'll do the "right thing." He'll come back to me because of the baby, even though he doesn't want it. He'll be terrified the entire time and our marriage will crumble anyway.

I'm not doing that to either of us.

"I'm here," Anna says as she jerks the curtain back. Her attention lands first on the nurse before moving to me freely crying. Her hand claps to her mouth. "Oh, God... did you...?"

She can't bring herself to ask, but I shake my head. "We haven't done the ultrasound yet. Wanted you to be here first."

I don't share with Anna my desire to have Van at my side. No sense in even going there.

In the end, I'm in the emergency room for almost four hours. The ultrasound was quick and I heard my baby's heartbeat as Anna squeezed my hand. The doctor assured me all was well. They wanted to x-ray my shoulder as the pain had increased and dark bruising started showing up. I declined but did have to wait for an orthopedist to examine it.

It was a long, exhausting ordeal, but I came out knowing the baby was okay. When we got home, Anna tried to get me to eat something but I was honestly exhausted. I wanted to go to sleep.

After she left, I trudged up the stairs, wanting the comfort of a mattress rather than the couch. The doctor said I could safely take Tylenol for the pain, but I didn't because it was bearable.

I got undressed, put on one of Van's T-shirts and fell into a deep sleep the minute my head hit the pillow.

CHAPTER 12

Van

AS I DRIVE by my house, I frown seeing that Simone's car isn't parallel parked in front. I glance to the other side of the street, in my mirrors to see if I passed it.

Maybe she parked in the back alley by my single-car garage but that would be foolish. It's dark back there with only one streetlamp on the corner for the entire short street. I've never specifically told her not to park back there because I was trying not to initiate contact or show her my concern but I assumed she was smart enough not to. Plus, she's been parked out front every single day since arriving.

I circle the block and my frown deepens as I note Simone's car isn't there.

Which means she's not home, and that means she's out somewhere. My eyes drop to the dashboard clock. It's almost two a.m. I had a game in Atlanta tonight—an out-and-back—and my ass is dragging. I want nothing more than to pass out in my bed for some solid sleep, but

I'm so irritated by Simone not being here, I know sleep won't be in my future.

I park, close the garage behind me and walk through the door that leads into the backyard. All the homes here have stand-alone garages at the back of the property. Great to protect your car from the elements but sucks if you have to walk through the backyard in snow or rain. Luckily, there's no precipitation and it's a relatively mild evening in the upper forties. Despite the nice chill in the air, my blood is boiling as I slog up the steps to the kitchen door.

I'm just about to slip my key in the lock when a light comes on in the kitchen. Not the overhead light, but the one from the refrigerator door, and it illuminates Simone standing before it perusing the shelves, which would be empty except for the groceries she buys.

I go still, watching her. Her back is to me and it gives me the opportunity to drink her in. To watch her without her knowing. I spend so much time lately averting my gaze from her, this feels like a refreshing drink of water after being out in the sun all day.

She's wearing one of my T-shirts—Dartmouth Hockey—and it comes to mid-thigh, absolutely swallowing her up. Simone always wore my shirts at home and that strikes something deep within me.

Mostly, though, I'm relieved to see her standing there and not out with God knows who, doing God knows what. I know how fucked up that is since I've given her no reason to be at home waiting for me. Quite the opposite, I've pushed her away at every chance, except for that one mistake I made three nights ago when she came on my tongue.

My dick pulses just thinking about it.

Slipping my key in the lock, I turn it and Simone looks my way. She can see me clearly through the glass panes and with the porch light casting enough illumination. I can only see half her face from the glow of the refrigerator, the other side shadowed. I see enough, though, to know she doesn't smile at me or look in the mood to talk, and I'm not sure whether to be relieved.

Simone turns back to stare inside the fridge as I enter the house. I close and lock the door behind me and because she's usually all up in my space trying to get me to interact with her, I'm momentarily dumbfounded that she's ignoring me.

I can't fucking help myself. "What are you doing up?"

"I haven't eaten since breakfast," she replies, reaching in to grab some yogurt.

"Why not?" I wince internally, berating myself for asking the question. *Just walk away, Van.*

Simone moves over to the counter, sets the cup of yogurt down and rummages through a drawer for a spoon. Her back is to me. "Got in a car accident today.

By the time I got home from the emergency room I was exhausted so I went to sleep. Just woke up."

She says it all so blandly, like it's not a big deal, but I feel like I'm about to blow a circuit.

"You were in a car accident?" I demand, flipping on the overhead light. "Are you okay?"

She turns to glance at me over her shoulder, her fingers working at tearing the top off the yogurt. "Just banged up a bit, but I'm fine. The car, not so much."

"Jesus Christ," I mutter as I toss my keys down and drop my duffel on the floor. I move to her, letting my eyes run over what visible skin I can see.

And right there, her left elbow is mottled black and blue. Carefully, I take her arm to examine it. "Is this it?"

She leans to the side, glances down at her left leg and lifts the T-shirt to reveal a bruise on her hip. "I got hit in the driver's side door by a truck. Just a few bruises. Nothing broken."

"No one called me." I'm not sure why that bothers me, but it does.

She shrugs without explaining why I was left in the dark. Reluctantly, I let her arm go and she turns away. I'm puzzled that I'm not getting more from her. This is the perfect time for her to get attention from me because I'm obviously worried. She could milk this. Simone would merely need to tell me that she feels weird all over her body and I'd examine it to make sure the doctors didn't miss something. I'd fall for it, too, not just because I will love her until my dying day, but because after touching her the other night, all I can think about is getting my hands on her again. The proximity to her right now has me half-hard.

Why the hell isn't she using this against me?

"You're sure you're okay?" I press.

"Fine," she murmurs, dipping her spoon into the yogurt and staring down at the container as she brings it to her mouth.

I study her, trying to find something in her words—or lack thereof—to get my bearings.

"I don't buy it," I snap and that causes her head to jerk my way. "You've been all over me the last two weeks, trying to wear me down, and now you've got me as a captive audience because I want to know if you're okay, you're going silent? What the fuck is the game, Simone?"

I get a rise out of her, and maybe that's what I was going for because as her eyes narrow, a thrilling rush sweeps through me to have her attention. It's fucked, but my cock steps up to the plate, stiffening with the desire to play.

Christ… I have to be cracked in the head trying to provoke her, but I stand my ground. In fact, I poke her even more.

Crossing my arms over my chest, I attempt a scathing glance down her body. "Is that your play, Simone? Be here waiting for me in a T-shirt and probably some skimpy panties on underneath—"

"—not wearing any panties," she says quietly and I almost falter.

Almost.

"Making me feel sorry for you because you were in an accident? Few bumps and bruises and you, what… think I'm going to go all soft and tender on you?"

I know the words coming out of my mouth are as ridiculous as they sound and Simone must think even more so because she tosses her spoon on the counter before taking two steps to come toe to toe with me.

I don't give her a chance to talk, though, goading her further. "Think wearing my T-shirt and telling me you're not wearing panties is going to break me? Is that what you think, baby? That I'll fall to this mental manipulation and fuck you?"

Simone scoffs, rolling her eyes. "Honestly, Van… I'm not sure you'd even know what to do with it if I were naked and sopping wet for you. I kind of understand what you mean by the shine wearing off. Not sure you'd even do it for me."

Okay, I know I brought that on, but fuck if she didn't just shred my man card. In all of her bratty glory over the years, Simone has never implied, inferred or come right out and alleged that I couldn't satisfy her.

And while deep down I recognize her machinations, I'll admit she just struck hard and deep.

I walk into her, causing her to back up until I walk her right into the center island. Reminiscent of the other night, I have her pinned. I rest a hand on the counter and push the other one right between her legs.

She wasn't lying about not having on panties and because I could find her pussy in the pitchest of black, my fingers immediately discover she is indeed sopping.

A low growl bubbles in my chest and I can't fucking help myself. I slowly press my finger inside her, all the while staring at her as it sinks in. Her eyes stay locked on mine but when I'm in to the third knuckle, they flutter closed and her hips rock.

"I know what to do with this," I say, my voice husky with pure lust for this woman.

"Prove it." She stares at me with defiant challenge.

Later, after I come down off my orgasm, I'm going to berate myself for this utter lack of strength and conviction. I'll call myself ten times a fool and I'll be even more of an ass to Simone to make up for giving in, but that will all come later.

Right now, I'm going to prove it.

I lean in and catch her bottom lip with my teeth, causing her to gasp with surprise. I bite it lightly and then lick it before sweeping my tongue inside her mouth. She moans as I deepen the kiss and her knees nearly buckle as I circle the wet tip of my finger around her clit.

Having decided to fuck my wife, I'm almost delirious with lust. I feel like a randy teenager getting ready to lose my virginity, having had nothing but my fist and dirty fantasies of Simone.

"Get my cock out," I rasp into her mouth.

Simone is the most sexually adventurous woman I've ever known and she doesn't have a shy bone in her body. She knows my body as well as I know hers, and she's a pure genius at undoing my pants. This isn't the first time we've both been swept up into a cyclone of desperate need.

I press two fingers back into her and she barely falters while unzipping my pants. She multitasks, rotating her hips as she releases my dick from its prison. I kiss her hard, one hand working between her legs and the other coming up to pinch a nipple. Simone moans and jerks but all the while, she fists my cock and gives me long, sure strokes that have me practically seeing stars. I don't want to come like a schoolboy, so I bat her hands away from me and use the time to whip off her T-shirt. I kiss my way down her neck, flick my tongue over her nipples and start to lower myself back into the same position I was in the other night. Going to lick her straight to a hot orgasm, then I'm going to fuck my wife, followed by some self-loathing and confusion.

"No," Simone says, a hand to my cheek to stop my

progress. She looks worried about something. "Just fuck me, Van. I don't need that."

Need it? Who cares if she needs it? I want to give it.

"I just want you inside me right now," she says, and while her words trail off, I can read between the lines.

Before I change my mind.

I surge upward, taking Simone with me. My hands go under her ass and her legs wrap around my waist. Our mouths fuse and I consider my options. Too far to her bedroom or mine, so I spin us around and pin her against the refrigerator.

I keep one hand on her bottom, the other sliding into her hair to hold her captive. My mouth works against hers, our tongues tangling, and Simone writhes in my arms. Her pussy rubs back and forth over my cock, driving me fucking mad with the need to be inside her.

We know each other so well and have fucked in every position imaginable that using touch and instinct alone, the head of my dick finds itself at her wet entrance. There's been virtually no foreplay—at least not the physical kind. Our sparring and anger have done enough to get us worked up.

I flex my hips and Simone pushes downward, sinking onto my shaft with exquisite slowness. Air hisses through my teeth and I can't concentrate on her mouth.

"Christ," I groan, resting my cheek against hers. I shake my head slowly… a pathetic attempt to deny that I don't want to do this.

Simone stills but wraps her arms around my neck, sliding her fingers into my hair. She puts her mouth near my ear and whispers, "Give it to me, Van. I promise I won't throw it in your face later and you can go back to ignoring me if you want."

I hesitate only a fraction of a second before I remember I already made peace with myself for this mistake. I punch my hips forward, slamming the rest of the way into her, and Simone lets out a cry of pleasure. My move is so forceful, the refrigerator shifts and I can hear the contents inside getting tossed about.

Wheeling around, I move for the table. It's sturdy-looking enough and better yet, there's nothing on top of it. I kick a chair out of the way and lay Simone on it, not once disrupting my place within her.

When her back is flat against the thick wooden surface, I pound away. It's without finesse and there are no sweet, filthy words that I would normally give her. She wanted to be fucked and I want to fuck her.

That's it.

CHAPTER 13

Simone

V AN MOVES INSIDE my body, snarling rumbles of need coursing through him so hard I feel it vibrating into me. He pulls out and slams back in, banging the table into the wall. He hikes my right leg up over his hip for more leverage, driving into me over and over again.

I want him to kiss me but I'm afraid to demand it. I'm afraid to do anything to disrupt this man who is being reminded right at this moment why he can't ever leave me.

He can't give this up.

Driving his hips against me, he hits something that only Van has ever been able to reach. Oh, I'm sure it's a physical thing but it's mostly emotional. When Van loses control while inside me, it's a primal claiming of my soul and that turns me on more than anything he could ever do. His moans and grunts telling me just how good—no, how perfect—I feel to him sends me into that free fall of ecstasy. An intense orgasm rips through me and it comes on so unexpectedly that I cry out my husband's name. It sounds like a prayer of worship.

Van groans and thrusts into me faster.

My body is still shuddering through the last vestiges of my own release when I take note that my husband is on the verge of tipping. I know all the signs... how he holds his breath and all sounds of pleasure go utterly silent. It's as if he's bracing himself to get wrecked and I know he's only seconds away from joining me—

"Fuck," he roars, pulling out of me so fast, I don't know what's happening. Van leans over me, planting a palm beside my head on the table and uses his other hand to jack his cock. I stare wide-eyed with confusion as he curses through his release, jetting all over my stomach. Van's face screws up and I'm not sure if it's pleasure or pain I'm seeing.

"Fuck," he huffs out, his favorite word to use that could mean any number of emotions. His hand twists on his cock, wringing out a few more drops of semen before falling away.

"Why did you pull out?" I ask with a frown as he straightens up, his chest rising and falling from the exertion of what we just did. Don't get me wrong... my husband has marked me many times over the years, but this wasn't that.

"Don't want you to get pregnant," he says flatly and once again I'm in the cold, dark world of Van Turner.

His head drops, refusing to look me in the eye as he tucks himself back into his pants and zips up.

Van turns to the kitchen sink to wash his hands while I lie like a useless lump, splayed out on the kitchen table. His semen puddled on my belly seems wrong and I realize, that was the most unsatisfying sex I believe I've ever had, despite the fact I got off. Those moments of pleasure that wracked my body just moments ago seem so very wrong.

I push up off the table and Van twists to look over his shoulder at me. I bend over to grab his T-shirt from the floor and wipe the fluid from my stomach. I drop it just as quickly and run out of the kitchen, through the living room and up the stairs into the guest bathroom. I turn the shower on and when the water's hot enough, I step in and wash myself clean. I put my face under the spray and let it take my tears down the drain. I'm despondent because the one thing I thought could still bond us seems broken too.

When I'm cried out, I wrap my hair in a towel, another around my body and cross the hall to the spare bedroom. I'll pull on warm pajamas and go to bed. I don't even have it in me to go sleep in the living room, just so I can have Van's attention. In fact, I think I decidedly don't want it tonight.

I pull up short, though, when I see Van sitting on the edge of my bed, waiting for me. His forearms are resting on his thighs and his head is hanging. It lifts when he hears me enter. "Are you okay?" he asks.

And God, does that make me so sad because I can hear so much love in his tone. It hurts the most to know he's leaving this marriage while still loving me to the depths of his soul.

"Yeah… I'm fine." *Lie.* "Just going to get dressed and go to bed."

Turning for my suitcase, I expect him to leave, but instead he says, "I didn't mean for that to happen."

"I know." I know while sex felt good for him, it was a line he didn't want to cross.

"I didn't mean to disrespect you," he says, punctuating the words so that I know he's clarifying something to me.

I turn to face him, gripping my towel tight around me like it's armor. I don't even know what to say.

"I'm tired of fighting, Simone." Van scrubs his hands over his face and I've never heard him sound more defeated. Even when all the shit went down three years ago with his dad, he never sounded this beaten down. "I'm tired of worrying about you. I'm tired of people asking me about my father. I'm tired of everything."

It occurs to me at this moment that ever since the book came out, Van and I have done nothing but fight. Heated arguments, yelling bouts and periods of cold silence. I'm not sure if we ever actually had a calm discussion.

I move to sit beside him on the bed and I take one of his hands in mine. "Tell me everything that's in your heart right now and I'll only listen. No fighting."

Van looks at me and I see all the love there. It's not something he has to prove to me. "I can't begin to describe to you what this is like for me. You know the facts, but you don't know the feelings. The things he wrote in that book…"

"You read it?" I ask in horror. Why would he do that to himself?

Van nods, gaze going down to the carpet. "I read enough and I want to vomit when I think about every person who read that book, and they're wondering… did I stick my hand in that nest and crush those eggs? Was I a little killer in the making? Did I kill the neighborhood cats and was I really a chip off the old block?"

"No one would ever believe that, Van. That book comes across as nothing but lies. You have a successful career, a family who loves you and a network of friends who know the real you."

"There are many who will want to believe it, baby. Many do believe it and wonder if I'm a monster hiding in plain sight. We live in a world where people want to believe the worst about others. Reporters are always going to ask me about this and it's never going away."

Van rises from the bed, but not to leave the room.

He turns to face me, tucking his hands in his pockets. "I've got this recurring waking nightmare... I think about it all the time. I imagine we have a kid... a daughter, because that's what I want first. And she comes home from her first day of school, and you and I are waiting for her to get off the bus. But instead of her running toward us with smiles, she's crying, because some kid at school told her that her grandpa was a serial killer." Van's voice cracks and he shakes his head. "I just can't do it. I suffered through it myself as a kid, but I was lucky. Etta took me away and gave me a new name, a new life. Our kids can't escape it, so I have to do the next best thing and refuse to bring children into this freak show. And I know you've said you can do without children to stay with me, but I can't do that to you, Simone. You are built to love and there are some lucky souls out there just waiting to be born so you can be their mother. I can't let you give that up. I won't let you give that up."

This is the point where I normally would argue with him, but for once, I'm not going to. I want him to know I hear him. That I understand.

I push up from the bed and move to my husband. I don't care if he likes it or not, but I press into his body and wrap my arms around him for a hug. I turn my cheek and press it to his chest. "I'm sorry, baby. I wish I could make that all better for you and I know I can't."

And for the first time since we separated, Van touches me with care and tenderness. He accepts my empathy. He wraps his arms around me and reciprocates the hug.

It doesn't last long... only seconds, but it makes up for that shitty sex we just had. And it gives me hope.

But he does pull away and when he does, I don't like the look on his face. "I'm going to move into a hotel."

"Why?" I exclaim, panic taking over.

"Because I can't be near you and stay true to my convictions. You're too much of a temptation and I'm not talking about sex. I'm talking about the fact that you represent too much hope and honestly, babe... it hurts to have it right now. I just want to be done with this." Van turns for the door but before he walks out, he says, "You know I love you, right?"

"I know."

"It's because I love you so much that I'm doing this."

"It's a mistake," I whisper.

He glances back at me. "It's a risk I'm willing to take."

Van slips out the door and I sit on the bed. My mind is already spinning... processing everything that happened tonight. Surely there is something I'm missing... some logical piece of information that will help me change his mind.

I know that Van thinks he just laid down the law, but I can't give up yet. There has to be a way to save my marriage.

Or the alternative, I need to let him go and hope he can figure it out on his own.

CHAPTER 14

Van

THE COLD FURY are already on the ice for pregame warmups when the Titans step out. I follow Boone, skating in a clockwise circle on our half of the arena. Rob Zombie's "Dragula" blares and fans line up at the glass behind the net with signs that say "Drake… I want to have your baby" and "Titans Don't Puck Around."

I skate slowly, my legs already limber and warm from riding a stationary bike and doing stretches a bit ago. Eventually, our team lines up for two-on-one drills, lobbing easy pucks at Drake to get him in the zone.

As I stand at the rear of the left-hand line near center ice, someone bumps me hard in the back. I turn to see Lucas standing there.

Even though I was with his sister for three years, two of which we've been married, Lucas is the one brother who never fully warmed up to me. He's genial enough at family gatherings but I don't know that he's ever forgiven me for the fact that I started seeing his baby sister right under his nose while we lived in the same house. This, despite the fact that his sister is the one who relentlessly came on to me.

From the very start, she was unrelenting in her flirting. She made comments about the way I looked or how I acted that threw me off because there was nothing coy about how she did it. She called it like she saw it.

"Hmmm," she said on the very first day we met, her tone suggesting she was trying to figure me out since I'd been pretty standoffish. "I'm going to go with brooding. It's a better fit for the hotness you exude."

What the fuck was she even talking about?

"Hotness?" I was at a loss as to how to deal with a woman who said things I didn't understand.

"Oh, come on." She let her gaze roam brazenly up and down my body before smirking at me. "Just look at all you got going on. All big and muscley. And those deep, sensitive eyes filled with mystery. Total hotness and totally broody."

I tried to pay her no mind. Ignored her, actually. And yet deep down, I knew that I was going to be in trouble where she was concerned.

Lucas jolts me out of my memories. "Going to kill you tonight," he says in a low voice, and he's not joking. The words are stone cold and laced with malice.

"Good thing we're not on the same lines, then," I mutter before turning away. No way am I going to fight her brother, especially not during an important game that has playoff-standing ramifications.

Lucas sneers. "On or off the ice, doesn't matter when."

"Whatever." I skate away from my brother-in-law and join the line on the opposite side. I scan the crowd. I don't know where she is, but there's no doubt Simone is here watching. She wouldn't miss a chance to see Lucas and Max play.

I don't think she'd be here to see me, not after the way I left her last night. There was a finality to our encounter and I know that because she listened to me. Heard how I felt.

Chose not to contradict me, fight for me or attempt to offer hope.

I told her I was moving out and she let me. I packed a bag and when I walked out the door, Simone was nowhere to be seen. Presumably up in the guest room, going to sleep.

She let me go.

I know I'm supposed to be glad it's over. Simone is free to get a new life. To have the happiness she deserves. It's everything I've reached for since that book came out.

And yet… there's not one part of me that has any relief from this overwhelming sensation of doom. If anything, I feel worse.

Simone told me I was making a mistake.

Did I?

"You good, man?" I glance over my shoulder and see Boone. "Saw you talking to Fournier."

"Yeah, all good." Boone knows I want a divorce from Simone, and everyone knows she's the little sister to Max and Lucas Fournier.

Boone taps his stick against the side of my leg. "Got your back, anyway."

I lift my chin, acknowledging the offer. Not the first time he's told me that, and there's not a doubt in my mind if Lucas somehow ends up on the ice at the same time as me and comes after me, my teammates will be right there. Hell, they all know about my troubles with Simone as word travels through the grapevine and most of them were privy to her attacking that fan at Mario's. But I haven't divulged details to any of them, nor do they know the reasons for us separating. It's obvious the stress of Arco's biography is a weight on me but no one really knows how that led to me leaving Simone.

I move along with the line, lost in my thoughts. I run a drill and when I'm finished, I search for Lucas on his side of the ice before choosing the next line. I'll keep distance between us. I'd already hurt his sister once. Like many couples do, we had a make-or-break moment when it first hit the news that Arco was my father. Simone wanted to stand by my side, but our relationship was too fucking new and I was too unsure of myself to accept what she was so freely giving to me. I had no confidence in what we had.

A freelance reporter who recognized me that one time I visited Arco in prison wrote a sensationalized article revealing my true identity to the world, just as the Cold Fury were starting their championship run. The article was entitled "The Unknown Madness of Van Turner," and it was the third-most horrific thing that had ever happened to me. The first, learning my dad was a serial killer, and the second, finding my mother's body after she died by suicide.

Simone was in California with me for the game and she immediately kicked into caregiver mode. She knew about Arco and she was my stalwart champion. Except when she asked, "What are we going to do?" my response was to immediately push her away.

"We?" I scoffed. "Why is this a we thing? Last I heard, your dad was a prominent doctor, not a serial killer." That didn't anger her. I had her empathy and it made me feel even worse. "I need you to stay out of this. It's hard enough to deal with the fallout of all this shit, but I don't need to worry about you at the same time."

Simone didn't back down. "You don't need to worry about me."

"You see, but I will. And fuck... it's hard work just letting you in. I'm constantly judging my actions and trying to figure out if they measure up to what I think are acceptable standards for you. And while I'm worrying about that shit with you, I've now got to deal with the entire world

knowing about my shame."

Simone frowned. "*Your shame?*"

"*Yes, my fucking shame,*" I yelled at her. "*Do you know how dirty and disgusting this shit makes me feel? I'm swept up into his sickness just by association. How many people are looking at me and wondering is he like his father?*"

In hindsight, I'm sure it wasn't what I thought, but at that moment, I thought she looked at me with pity and I couldn't take it. I tried to leave… put space between us.

She begged me not to push her away. "*I've got your back.*"

I snarled at her. "*You've got my back? You've got my back?*"

She lifted her chin and stood her ground. "*I do.*"

Disdain was evident in the scathing timbre of my tone. "*And just how do you have my back, Simone? Just how are you going to support me through this?*"

"*By standing beside you. By defending you. By telling and showing the world that you're kind and generous and loving and—*"

"*I fuck you, Simone.*" *My tone was flat and without any tenderness.* "*I give you orgasms. I laugh at your silliness. But I am not kind nor generous nor loving. So you'd essentially be lying on my behalf. Is that how you'll support me?*"

"*You're more than that,*" *she whispered.*

"*You know I'm not. And besides that, do you think people are going to accept what you're saying? I give a little interview with the media and proclaim I'm a good guy, but* instead the media shows highlights of all my fights to speculate that I'm a violent person. I know how this shit plays out. It's why it's easier to keep people out."

And still, she would not give up. She would not abandon me. Relentless brat that she was. "Van… I get you're angry, and maybe the natural thing is to drive away those that care about you—"

"You're wrong. I don't intend to drive Etta away at all." The implication was crystal clear that only Etta was welcome in my life. I'm not sure I really meant that but I was spiraling so quickly. I said the words even though they felt wrong. "I made a mistake. I should have never gotten in this deep with you. Should have never opened myself up like I did."

"Sounds like you're blaming me for some reporter who wrote an article about you," she said, showing the first sign of anger.

"No, not blaming you. Just angry for taking myself off the radar to begin with."

Ultimately, that day ended with us parting ways. I told her I needed time and maybe later… after I got through the playoffs, we could… I'm not sure what.

Simone was having none of it. A backbone of solid steel, she wasn't going to let me string her along. "That's not how this works. There is no later. It's either now—when you need me the most in your life—or not fucking ever."

The dumbest words I'd ever issued in my life came tumbling out. "Then it's not fucking ever."

She left California and we were done.

Not forever, though. I realized how stupid I had been and there was a hell of a lot of apologizing for the way I hurt her. I was a lucky man she gave me another shot.

I force those memories away, but it's not lost on me that I'm repeating history. I've once again pushed her away and with any luck, she'll be heading back to Vermont sooner rather than later now that I've moved out of the house. The only difference between now and then is I have no intention of going after her to grovel.

When warm-ups are complete, we head back to the locker room for last-minute instructions from Coach West. I have to admit, his pep talks are really good. He's not the type of person who speaks because he likes to hear himself. He chooses only words that he knows will impact us and by the time we take the ice again for the start of the game, we're all fueled by hype and adrenaline.

From the first face-off, the energy in the arena is electric. The Cold Fury are at the top of their division, same as us. They're striving to take back the championship rights from the Arizona Vengeance, who won the last two years. We're a cobbled-together Cinderella team that no one thought would be this good.

It's late in the first period when there's a line shift and I'm back on the ice with Mason, Dillon, Evgeny and Anders. We're getting more in sync with each passing day and we transition smoothly, right into the defensive zone.

Anders takes point, Evgeny on the left and Dillon on the right. Mason and I split the defense and I station in front of the net, trying to block Max Fournier's field of vision.

That's when I see him.

Lucas is out on the ice, which hasn't happened yet and he's not out playing with his regular line. I'm not sure if he came out on his own or if his coach sent him, but when our eyes make contact, I know he's going to take a shot at me.

It happens when the puck gets caught up on the boards right behind the net. I get to it first, but then I'm slammed into from behind, a stick jamming painfully in my mid-back. The puck is at my skates and I'm trying to knock it loose, but Lucas is tying me up.

"Come on, asshole. Let's me and you have a go," he snarks as his stick chops at my skates in what looks like a reasonable attempt to free the puck, but he catches my leg and it fucking hurts.

I toss an elbow back at him and it connects. He shoves me against the boards. "Can't wait for Simone to be done with you. Get herself a real man. Someone who's not a pansy-ass."

Rage flows through my veins and I spin on him. Lucas smiles with triumph, immediately tosses his gloves to the ice and pulls up one sweater sleeve, then the other.

It's the universal sign that he's ready to go and I have no choice but to drop my own gloves.

The crowd roars its approval, not just because their new defenseman has quite the record of pounding other players into the ground, but because everyone knows we're brothers-in-law. Granted, no one knows the animosity.

The rest of the team stays clear, as do the refs, letting us have a go.

We circle each other to the left of the net and as if by some pre-planned moment, we crash into each other. We're both seasoned fighters and I know his style well since we were defensive line mates together for the Cold Fury. Normally, I'd say I'm the meaner of the two and that gives me the advantage, but Lucas is riding his heroic white steed tonight, trying to avenge his sister.

I grab his sweater at his chest and throw a quick right cross. It glances off Lucas's helmet but he strikes fast, his fist at my left cheek, hitting me so hard I feel the skin tear. I pull back my arm and let it fly, landing two solid hits to his head, although still mostly helmet. I'm pulling back for a third when something slams into me from the side so hard, my skates go out from under me. I hit the ice with a jarring impact and a huge body lands right on top of me, knocking the air from my lungs. I focus and see it's Max looking at me through his goalie mask before he's pulled off by the refs.

I jump up, ready to go at Lucas again but see that both teams have mobbed each other, having taken offense to Max jumping into the fight. There's a lot of shoving and cursing, name-calling and dares to drop gloves. Eventually, the refs get players sent back to their respective benches, and all the while, the crowd screams for blood. The Titans' fans are not happy I got double-teamed, but none of them know I had that coming.

I skate to the bench while the melee is being sorted out and let one of the trainers slap two butterflies on the cheek wound. I then immediately skate toward the penalty box.

Lucas is already sitting in his little glass prison, hatred radiating from his expression as he watches me. We're both given five-minute major penalties for fighting and to my surprise, Max is given one too. He doesn't serve the penalty, though, but rather a player of their coach's choosing joins Lucas.

This is fortuitous as it puts us up a player, and with the advantage, we capitalize when Foster scores a goal just eighteen seconds into the power play. When our penalties are up and we come out of our respective boxes, I dig the knife in just a bit as Lucas and I skate past each other. "Thanks for the goal."

♦

WE'RE ALL RIDING high after defeating the Cold Fury, so

much so that I've been able to put Simone out of my mind for a good half hour while I shower and change. I've enjoyed the recaps of great plays, snapping towels on asses and the boisterous vibe going on.

"Van," Boone calls out as I gather my duffel and head for the exit. "Mario's. Meet you there for a beer?"

I shake my head. "I'm out, man. Going home to bed. I'm exhausted."

Of course, going home means going to the hotel I checked into.

"Old man," he taunts, and I don't let it get to me.

I throw a hand up in the air. "See you at practice tomorrow."

I leave the good vibes and excited banter behind, stepping out into the hallway, and come up short as I see Max waiting there. He's clearly fresh out of the shower with his dark hair the same color as Simone's wet and his hazel eyes staring at me warily. He's in street clothes and not a suit, and that means he must be staying here in Pittsburgh for the night. I presume to visit with Simone and Malik.

"Here for round two?" I ask as I move past him and head toward the players' entrance into the parking garage.

"You're welcome, by the way," he replies as he follows me.

That stops me and I turn to face him. "What should

I be thanking you for?"

"For stopping Lucas from killing you. It's why I took you down to the ice so the refs would stop the fight."

Huh? So he wasn't trying to kill me along with his brother. Interesting.

I shrug and turn away. "Well, thanks."

"Come on, man," Max says, jogging past me and getting in my way so I'm brought up short. "Give me five minutes of your time to talk about Simone."

"What's to talk about? I've asked for a divorce, she's clinging on without any hope. Lucas and Malik hate me. So should you."

"But does Simone?" Max asks pointedly.

I don't even think to lie to him. "No. She still loves me."

"And you still love her."

"Always," I admit with no shame. "Which is why she can't be with me."

Max lowers his gaze, shaking his head with a smirk plastered on his face.

"What?" I demand with irritation. Like he has the most obvious answer and I can't see it.

"I'm going to make a prediction," Max says with a chuckle as he steps in and claps a hand on my shoulder. I stare at him, teeth clenched. "I predict that everything is going to turn out just fine."

Meaning that Simone will move on and have a wonderful and fulfilled life without me? "What makes you say that?"

"Because you both love each other," he replies, letting his hand fall away. "You can't love each other like that and let it go."

"Why is everyone so insistently ignoring the fact that I am, in fact, letting her go, despite being in love with her? I've made my decision. It's done."

"If you say so," Max says with a grin. "But I predict you'll wise up because you'll have faith that you and Simone can handle anything as long as you're together, and I also have complete confidence that my sister will welcome you back with open arms. She did it once before, remember?"

Yeah... I remember. She was too good a woman for me and still is, for that matter.

"Good luck," Max says, pivoting and walking away. He takes three paces and then turns to face me, as if he has just one more thing to say. "Oh, and see you at the next family get-together."

I snort because that's ridiculous. "Whatever."

CHAPTER 15

Simone

A NNA KISSES MALIK on his neck before she pushes up off the love seat. "I'm exhausted and going to bed. Love you."

"Love you back." Malik holds on to her hand until their arms stretch and fingers slide against each other before breaking apart.

"Good night, Anna," I say, and Lucas and Max echo me.

When the door to the master bedroom closes, we're all silent for a moment. The Fournier siblings are all together in Malik and Anna's living room. They're staying the night and flying back commercial tomorrow, taking the opportunity to spend time here with us all in the same city. It's close to midnight, but I've got nowhere to be tomorrow. I decided to stay here tonight so we could all hang out as long as we wanted to.

I know Lucas and Max are exhausted as they played a well-fought game. Lucas is currently sprawled out on the big couch and I'm sitting on the floor with my back resting against it near his feet. Max is cocked back in the recliner and Malik is still sunk into the love seat Anna just vacated.

"Get me a beer, runt," Lucas demands, moving his knee to bump me in the back of my head. He's got two empties sitting on the coffee table.

"Bite me," I reply.

"Twerp." Lucas swings his legs over my head and rolls off the couch. "Anyone else want one?"

"I'll take another," Max says, draining the last of his bottle.

Malik lifts his chin. "Me too."

"Sis?" Lucas inquires.

I hold up my bottle of water. "I'm good."

I'd told them earlier I had an upset stomach and wasn't in the mood to drink. I was patted on the head while they got busy with the beer. This is typical for a Fournier get-together. It's not often we're all under the same roof, but after the parents go to bed, the kids usually stay up late and talk. In the last handful of years, that's included significant others, but Max's wife, Jules, and Lucas's wife, Stephanie, stayed back in Raleigh with my adorably perfect nieces and nephews. And, of course, Van's not here.

No, he's holed up in a hotel somewhere, avoiding me.

When Lucas comes back in, he delivers each beer and

then plops onto the couch, but this time he doesn't lie down. He pats the available seat cushion. "Get your ass up here and let's talk."

It's not the offer to give up the hard floor that has me dubious, but the tone in his voice that sounds like this was preplanned.

I glance around, eyeballing Malik and Max, and yup… they're no longer casually slouched in their chairs but sitting up straight. Apparently, they've been waiting for Anna to go to bed to gang up on me about Van.

"Actually," I say as I stand, stretching and giving a huge fake yawn. "Kind of tired. I'm going to bed."

I try to walk past Lucas but he grabs the back of my shirt and slings me toward the seat next to him. I can't stop my momentum and the minute my butt hits the cushion he points at me. "Stay."

"Woof, woof," I mutter, but I stay. I scoot back into the corner of the couch and cross my legs. "But I'm going to talk first." I look pointedly at Lucas. "You're an asshole for fighting Van tonight."

"It's just hockey," he says smoothly.

"You're full of shit. Everyone saw you instigate it and it was uncalled for. Christ, Lucas… you split his cheek open."

"Max was in on it too," Lucas says petulantly. "Why am I the only one getting yelled at?"

I snort. "Because Max ended the fight."

Lucas's gaze snaps to Max and he narrows his eyes. "You weren't joining me to avenge our sister?"

"Sorry, dude," Max says, shaking his head. "I was stopping it and the only way was to get Van on the ground."

"You traitor," Lucas exclaims dramatically.

I blow Max a kiss. "It's why you're my favorite brother."

"Whatever." Lucas scoffs and faces me. "But now that we have you alone and can talk some sense into you, I want you to give Van the divorce he's seeking. He's killing you slowly... death by a thousand paper cuts. Can't stand the fucker and I say good riddance."

He doesn't elaborate but after that kind of statement, what more needs to be said? My head turns to Malik who I suspect has similar feelings.

Malik's expression is sympathetic, but he shrugs. "You tried, Simone. Now it's time to move on. While I love having you in the same city as me, you have a career back in Vermont that you should go back to. Dive into work. Take your mind off things."

"And divorce Van?" I ask for clarification.

While his expression is still soft in understanding, his nod is firm. "Yes. And divorce Van."

I swing my head toward Max, now perched on the edge of the recliner. He's got his elbows on his knees, beer bottle held loosely in one hand. "And what about you?" I ask.

"I want you to be happy."

"Me too," I say with a bitter laugh. "And to me, that's saving my marriage. Yet you want me to give up and not fight?"

Max nods at Malik and Lucas. "I agree with these bozos. I think you've done everything you can. I don't agree you should give up hope, but I think you should give up trying. Van knows how you feel. It's on him now."

Always the voice of reason. Lucas and Malik are the hotheads, but Max has always been so steady, you can't help but take his opinions seriously.

I grab a pillow and put it on my lap, tugging at the tasseled fringes. "I'm going to ask all three of you the same question and I want you to be honest with me."

"Shoot," Lucas says, draping his arm over the back of the couch and angling more my way.

I address him first as he's the most vocal about disliking my husband and he tried to beat the shit out of him on the ice tonight.

"Do you care about Arco's biography? Does that change how you view Van or feel about him?" Lucas opens his mouth to answer, but I hold my hand out. "And don't tell me you dislike or hate him, because I know damn well you don't. He was your teammate and he's your brother-in-law, and I've watched you two over

173

the years and—"

"Fine," Lucas says with a grimace. "Yes, I like Van. I'm pissed as hell at him though for even going where he went with you. He's disappointed me. And to answer your question, no, that shit doesn't bother me at all. Arco was a psychopath and anything he wrote in those journals that got turned into a book was probably done with the intent to manipulate perception. I mean, anyone who reads that shit can see he's just glorifying things in an attempt to torture Van long after the asshole kicked the bucket."

"You read the book?" I ask, completely incredulous. Lucas hates reading.

"Of course I did. I wanted to be able to defend him if someone said something to me about it."

Tears prick at my eyes over how thoughtful that was.

"We all read it," Max says, and my head turns his way. "Even Mom and Dad, and we all discussed it."

My jaw drops. "Without me?"

"You had enough on your plate," Malik says, drawing my attention. "All of us think it's horseshit, by the way."

"And have any of you actually said that to Van?"

Utter silence. They glance at one another, then at me with guilt-ridden expressions.

"Jesus," I mutter, taking the pillow and slinging it hard and fast at Lucas. It catches him in the face and beer spews out of his bottle all over his shirt. "You couldn't have taken five minutes of your time to reach out to your brother-in-law to tell him not to worry about it? That it came across as kooky? That you had his back?"

"We just assumed he would know that," Malik says in defense of their inaction. "The stuff in that book about Van was so ludicrous, I honestly didn't think it even required me saying I didn't believe it."

I throw my hands in the air. "And here we are… I'm on the brink of divorce, you jerks are trying to beat Van up and telling me you hate him, and not one of you tried to support him."

More silence. They all look regretful, I'll give them that.

"I have a question for you," Malik says. "Why is this upsetting Van so much? I mean, I get there are horrible innuendos made and it's awful having a serial killer as a father, people wondering if you got anything from him and all… but it's no different from what he went through three years ago when he was outed as Arco's son. There was an article and the press went nuts. All of his teammates stood by his side and no one believed the negative shit. So why now is this upsetting him to the point he wants to cut you loose? It makes no sense."

I hadn't wanted this to come up, but it has, and I can't lie to my brothers. I also want them to not be disappointed in Van. I want them to understand that his feelings and emotions are legitimate and must be given credence, even if none of us like the way he's handling things. "Van and I had been trying to get pregnant when the book came out."

"I didn't know that," Lucas exclaims and looks to Max and Malik. "Did y'all know that?"

I don't give them a chance to respond. "We didn't tell anyone we were trying. Didn't want the pressure of all you busybodies checking in all the time, asking if I was knocked up." None of them have a rejoinder to that, so I continue. "But to answer your question why Van was so upset, he couldn't see past his children having to live with this stigma. He didn't want them to suffer the same embarrassment or bullying he had to endure. The book was a lot different than just being outed as the son of a serial killer. That book told lies about Van that he'd have to defend and he doesn't mind taking that on for himself. But he didn't want our kids to have to suffer so he changed his mind, doesn't want to have kids and asked for a divorce."

"Okay," Max says with a nod. "I can accept not wanting to have kids—which would be a huge point of contention in your marriage—but why a divorce? Y'all could have put the subject of kids on the back burner or—"

"I told him I would stay with him even if we didn't have kids," I pipe in.

Max points at me. "There… that's how you handle things by compromising or waiting for things to clear, so why ask you for a divorce?"

"He's got someone on the side," Lucas snarls. "I bet—"

"No, he doesn't," I say with a glare that has him snapping his mouth shut. "Van loves me, but in his mind, I deserve to have children. He thinks by letting me go, he's giving me my best shot at happiness. That I'll have a more fulfilled life without him."

"That's the dumbest thing I've ever heard," Malik mutters.

"It's not," I say sadly. "He and I talked the other day and I really listened to him. He's not taking this lightly. He's thought this out and he feels this is for the best. While I disagree with him, I can't diminish his feelings."

"I still say it's stupid," Malik says.

Lucas nods. "So stupid."

I glance at Max. "What's your take?"

"Stupid," he concurs. "But I honestly think things will work out. I think Van is jammed up with emotions and can't reason through this. I think you should leave him alone and go home. Let him figure this out because if you goad him into anything, you'll never know if he wants a life with you."

That gives me pause. I had an ace in the hole. I'd been considering telling Van I'm pregnant and I know that would force him back into a marriage with me. He'd do the honorable thing ultimately. But Max is right... would that really be enough? If he was forced to do it?

I can't do that to him. I can't do that to myself. I'm going to keep the pregnancy a secret for a while and I'll just have to see what Van decides to do.

I'm suddenly more than exhausted. I stretch my legs and scoot off the couch. "I'm really going to bed now."

When I stand, I walk around the room and give each of my brother's a hug, telling them I love them. They reciprocate, as they always do. We Fourniers love each other fiercely.

When I reach the staircase, I look back to find them all staring at me with tender expressions. My gaze stays on Max. "You think Van will come through on this?"

"I do," he says.

For the first time since I arrived in Pittsburgh, a tiny flicker of hope burns in the center of my chest. I'm not going to fan it to flame just yet, but it's enough to tide me over for a while.

CHAPTER 16

Van

I'M NOT SURE if this is a good idea, but I'm committed now. I follow Boone and Drake into the UPMC Children's Hospital, a photographer and two Titans' staff members right behind us. We're here to visit the inpatient kids to dole out jerseys and signed sticks in an effort to brighten their day.

Boone set this up and I was surprised to learn that he visits the hospital a lot in his free time. He approached Brienne about having the Titans sponsor visits and publicize it to help raise money to offset the cost of medical expenses some families can't afford.

It's a fucking brilliant idea but not something I would've necessarily done on my own had he not invited me. It's better than sitting in my hotel room today, moping about my broken marriage and my serial killer father.

Boone is arranging for all of our teammates to take turns with him but I got the first invite and Drake pulled rank, being the fiancé of the team owner, and got in on today's visit.

We're greeted by some hospital executive whose name I didn't catch and we pose for pictures in the lobby. Then Boone leads us to the elevator and stops on the fourth floor. Today's agenda includes the oncology ward and honestly, I'm a bit terrified to see kids with cancer. I'm sensitive to the idea of children, anyway, but visiting those in pain or potentially dying has got my stomach tight with anxiety.

Boone seems at ease, though, waving to nurses and doctors we pass, and then he's entering the first room.

"Aiden, my man." Boone's voice is affectionate and as I follow him in, I see a boy sitting up cross-legged in his bed. He's bald and thin except for his face, which looks slightly swollen. He's hooked up to an IV and is extremely pale with dark circles under his eyes.

His face lights up when he sees Boone though. Drake and I hang back near the door as Boone offers his hand to the kid and they do a half handshake, half hug as Boone bends over the bed. When he pulls back, he turns and points at us. "Brought some friends."

Aiden's mouth drops open when he sees us. "Holy shit—"

"Hey, hey… language," Boone warns.

"Holy crap," Aiden amends and slowly swings his legs out of the bed. He's wearing a pair of sweatpants, a T-shirt and those hospital socks with grips on the bottom. He maneuvers the IV tube out of the way like he's had lots of experience and grabs hold of the pole from where the medicine hangs, moving it across the room toward us with shuffling steps.

Drake moves first, holding out his fist, and the kid bumps it with his own. Then he turns to me and I offer the same.

"Drake McGinn and Van Turner." The kid shakes his head in awe. "I can't believe you're here... in my room."

Boone gives Aiden a faux glare. "You never get that excited when I come to visit."

Aiden shoots him a grin. "I see you a lot."

"The specialness has worn off, hasn't it?" Boone teases.

My stomach churns, thinking of the way I've told Simone she's no longer shiny to me. She knows it's a lie, right? Formulated specifically to make her mad enough to leave me but never in a million years could that woman ever be anything less than pure brilliance.

"We brought some gifts," Drake says, and he motions one of the staffers into the room and the photographer enters as well. "Can we get some pictures with you? Probably make the front page of the sports section."

"Hell yeah," Aiden exclaims, then ducks his head when Boone gives him a disapproving look. "I mean, heck yeah."

I'm intrigued by Boone and the way this kid knows him so well. I wonder if he's this close to all the kids he visits.

We spend about five minutes talking to Aiden. He's given a Highsmith jersey after he admits Coen is his favorite player, but he asks the three of us to sign it. Drake also gives him a goalie stick with his signature on it.

We pose for photos, including some with Aiden's phone. "My dad's going to die that he missed this," he quips, scrolling through the photos after his phone is handed back to him.

"Listen… got a lot more kids to see," Boone says as he motions for Aiden to get back in bed. "I'll see you Sunday."

Aiden radiates an energy that wasn't there when we first walked in. "Really?"

"Really," Boone says and then hugs the boy. "Gotta give you extra good luck before your transplant, right?"

Transplant? Jesus… the things these kids go through.

We move right to the next room and Boone goes in first. "Amelia… my little princess," he calls out.

Christ… does he know all the kids in this ward? It's pretty fucking amazing, to be honest.

Drake and I follow him into the room and see a little girl no more than six or seven years old. She's completely bald like Aiden, rail thin and looks like she would blow over in a strong wind. As we enter, she's playing Candy Land with a man I'm guessing is her father.

Amelia looks really sick and I can see the stress lines on her father's face. I can't even imagine having a child with cancer or whatever she has. I don't know what any of these kids have, but they're obviously very ill.

The little girl squeals when she sees Boone and I note her dad has a genuine smile seeing his daughter light up like that. I suppose it's the small moments you cherish most.

I glance at Drake and we exchange a look. He's a dad and I can see it on his face… he'd go crazy if this happened to one of his boys.

We spend almost four hours at the hospital, visiting with kids and handing out Titans gear. We talk with parents, giving them a little respite from hovering over their ill children, and we thank doctors and nurses for their fine work. It's fulfilling and draining at the same time.

After we leave the hospital, we head to a bar for a few beers to decompress.

At a high top with a shared bowl of peanuts among us, I ask, "How often do you visit the hospital?"

He shrugs. "Once a week, sometimes more."

Drake shakes his head. "I don't know how you do it, man. I'm drained after seeing those sick kids for just a few hours."

"But don't you feel good in your soul?" Boone asks with a grin.

"I do," Drake admits.

I do too. I've felt like such a shit for all the stuff I've done to Simone, this was a bit of a balm to make kids smile all day.

"Kids are resilient as hell," Boone says. "We have a lot to learn from them."

"That's God's honest truth," Drake says. "My ex-wife has put my kids through hell and I still marvel at the way they're able to deal with it. Far better than I did."

This gets my attention. "What do you mean?"

I've come to know a little about Drake by talking to him and others on the team. I also remember when it was hot news, his wife accusing him of betting on games. All untrue, of course, but it was a lot of shit he went through.

Drake takes a sip of his beer. "She's a drug addict, so you never know what you're going to get with her. Whether she'll be high as a kite or in a depressive state or totally normal. My kids were always walking on eggshells around her. Always worried about what kind of mom she'd be. The last time she showed up, they were afraid of her."

"How did you protect them from that?"

Drake shrugs. "I realized pretty quickly I just

couldn't shield them completely, and to be honest, I'm glad I didn't. I had to guide them and teach them how to cope."

That seems impossible to me. "And how did you do that?"

I get a strange look from Drake as he grabs some peanuts. "You talk honestly to them. I kept it age-appropriate but I was transparent with them about the issues surrounding their mom. I guess I just taught them that they have no control over what she does and says—they can only stay true to themselves. They can only control how they react."

I'm stunned by how stoic he is about all this. It's horrific thinking of his boys dealing with a strung-out mother.

"It can't be that simple," I mutter, staring down at my beer.

"Fuck no, it's not simple," Drake says with a laugh. "It's hard work."

"But don't you worry about your kids being screwed up over the things they've seen and heard?"

Drake exchanges a look with Boone and it seems to convey that they both know my questions go beyond simple curiosities.

With his gaze coming back to me, Drake crosses his forearms on the table. "Let me tell you something, my friend. Children are the greatest gift any human can hope to have in their life. But it's a nonstop ride of worry that you're doing the right things, saying what they need to hear, protecting them when they can't for themselves, and letting them fall because they need to learn what that feels like, and even more... how to get back up again. Even as hard as it is, it's the absolute best thing you could ever hope to have in your life. It's worth all the pain and worry just to tuck them into bed at night and have them say *I love you, Daddy*."

My entire body flushes with warmth, a strange flood of regret mixed with a sudden awareness that I've just been clued into something very fucking important. So monumental, it could make me a happy man again.

All this time spent obsessing over the worst, I've never considered it could be okay. Or that there was a way to guide children through tough times. I never really had that. I mean... Etta... she just whisked me away and my life with her was idyllic. It never occurred to me that with the right parenting, a child could indeed handle ugly things.

I'm still not quite sure I'd be any good at talking to kids the way Drake does, but the one thing I know is that he's made me a bit more open-minded. It's not just black-and-white anymore.

"Sorry," I say as I rise from the table and nab my wallet from my back pocket. I drop a hundred-dollar bill on the table. "I gotta go. Drinks are on me."

Boone and Drake don't know the details of my woes with Simone or why we're separated. But I'm sure they're both smart enough to figure out that I just had an epiphany of some sort.

It takes all my effort not to speed on the thirty-minute drive to our house. I don't even bother parking in the back but slide into the parallel spot that Simone's car normally occupies. I make a mental note I need to find out the status of her car—whether it can be repaired—but that's not what's important right now.

I fly up the steps, fumble with the key in the lock and practically crash through the front door. I'm yelling her name as I disable the security alarm.

"Simone," I call out. She's not in the kitchen or living room. I bound up the stairs. "Simone."

When I turn into her room, I immediately know she's gone. The room is empty except for the furniture that was here when I moved in. Suitcase, clothes, shoes… all of it gone. Even the linens are stripped off the bed.

She's… gone.

I can't even begin to process it. The woman is the most relentless person I know. She doesn't ever give up in a fight, and the first time we broke up doesn't count. She didn't give up that time but rather gave me an ultimatum, which I didn't accept, so, in essence, I'm the one who gave up. I couldn't blame her for leaving that time.

But fuck... I kind of blame her now. Where is my hotheaded temptress who tries to seduce me back into being a husband? Or the woman who gets in my face and yells at how stupid I've been?

When Simone first found out about my dad, I panicked and tried to push her out of my life. Our relationship was new and I was so fucking ashamed of who I was.

"Just stay the fuck away from me," I snarled at her. All my walls were going back up, my instinct to protect myself overwhelming me.

Did she stay away? No.

She ran at me, her petite body slamming into mine, and she wrapped her arms around me tight. She clung to me, pressing her face into my chest, and squeezed me so tight I thought she'd crack a rib.

I didn't reciprocate the hug. I was frozen in fear.

"You better hold me, you motherfucker," she growled, and it was the fiercest, most intimidating thing anyone had ever said to me. "I know you, Van Turner. And I think you're mighty fine. Don't you even think about telling me I deserve better, or that you don't have anything to give me. At the very least, you better sure as fuck keep giving me what you've been giving me, and if I had my way, you'd talk to me and tell me everything."

That was probably the moment I fell a little in love with my wife. Demanding I give her what she deserved and feeling like I deserved her in return.

"I'm not surprised," I finally muttered, wrapping my arms around her.

She looked up at me. "By what?"

"That you won't take no for an answer. You're relent-less."

Where the hell did my brat go? There's no way she could have given up. It's not in her makeup.

I pull out my phone and call the one person I know will know where Simone is and who will be willing to talk to me.

Anna answers on the second ring. "Hi, Van."

"Where is she?" I ask.

"Who?"

"Don't play dumb blond with me, Anna. You're one of the smartest people I know."

Anna laughs. "She went back to Vermont."

Even though I knew that, it still fucking hurts to hear it. "But... why?"

"Probably because you're a big fucking dum-dum."

I nearly choke as I bark out a laugh, so surprised to hear Anna drop an f-bomb and *dum-dum* in the same sentence. "Yeah... that I am," I assure her. "When did she leave?"

"Night before last. Are you going to call her?"

"No," I reply and I hear a sharp gasp of dismay from Anna. "Calling won't be good enough. I'll need to grovel and that can only be done in person."

"But she's in Vermont. You're in Pittsburgh. You've got a home game tomorrow night."

That is indeed a problem. "I'll look into chartering a plane. It can't be more than a couple of hours' flight time. Surely I can fly there, win my wife back and get back home to Pittsburgh in twenty-four hours, right?"

Anna's silent a moment, then says, "If you can't find a private charter, call me back. I'll see if I can requisition one of Jameson's planes."

"Thanks, Anna." My voice is gruff with emotion that she's willing to help me out, especially since I know her husband wouldn't lift a pinkie finger. "I'll reach out to Brienne first to see if she's got some contacts, but I'll let you know if I run up against a wall."

"Good luck, Van. But something tells me you're not going to need it." She laughs to herself and adds, "I'd still grovel if I were you."

CHAPTER 17

Simone

P OKING AT THE burning logs in the fireplace, I watch the sparks fly upward, thinking they're hell's little fireflies. There's room for another log so I add one. We never go to sleep while a wood fire is still burning but I'm wide awake and know I can outlast it this evening.

The temperatures dipped way low tonight and I'm feeling the chill of the teen numbers outside. There's no shame when nine o'clock rolls around and I'm snug in my fleece pajamas and fuzzy socks, I make myself a cup of hot cocoa the best way… with heavy cream, sugar, Ghirardelli chocolate and a dash of cayenne pepper to warm me up from the inside. Van taught me how to make it that way and he learned it from Etta.

When I'm settled on the couch and holding the steaming mug before me, I look down at my belly and give it a slow rub. "Don't worry, little baby… I went light on the pepper. Still, I hope you come out as spicy as me."

I grin, thinking about all the ways my life is going to

change. My heart flutters sweetly when I think about all the love I have to give to this child.

What I don't think about is wondering if she'll have a dad. I know she will because I know Van won't abandon it. Now, whether our marriage can be repaired is another matter. This isn't the first time Van has gotten scared and his first reaction was to wall himself off. It might be that he's just not cut out to be everything I need and I'll have to come to grips with that.

But for now, I'm going to wait for him to work through this. I will give him the time he needs without me breathing down his neck or trying to force him to love me the way I want. If he can't come to terms with his demons, though, I'll tell him I'm pregnant and invite him to be involved in this journey as much or as little as he wants, but not as my husband. I'm not going to be in a marriage that is less than what I used to have with him.

I sip my cocoa and put it on the side table, nabbing the remote. I'll binge-watch some Netflix. Just as I'm about to turn on the TV, a flash of lights comes through the living room window, rolling through the room before cutting off. Someone just pulled into the driveway and my pulse starts to race. No one would be visiting me at his hour.

No one but…

No way.

I roll off the couch and walk to the front door that's

covered by a lacy curtain. I pull it aside and see a white sedan sitting behind my rental car. It's too shadowed to see clearly, but it's definitely a man who gets out and walks toward the porch.

And as he finally steps into the glow from the sconce beside the door, my breath freezes as I realize it's my husband wearing nothing but jeans and a long-sleeve T-shirt with a duffel slung over his shoulder.

Pressing my hand to my chest, I feel my heart in a mad gallop. I take a deep breath, unlock the door and swing it open just as he reaches the top step.

He halts, taking me in as frosty breath billows from his mouth, his eyes roaming slowly from my head to my feet, then back up to tether to my face. He says nothing, but neither do I. There's no tension, though... which is weird. It's almost like he's supposed to be here right at this moment and I have no clue why, but I'm also not surprised.

I can only think back to Max saying he believed everything would work out okay and I guess deep down... I believed him.

"I'm going to grovel," Van announces as he drops the duffel and moves toward me. "But first... I just want to hug you."

There's never a moment that runs through my mind to deny him. I gladly let him walk his body right into mine, wrap me in those strong arms and hold me tight to his chest as he presses his cheek to my head. I burrow into him, listening to his heartbeat, which is slow and steady compared to mine. I don't even feel the cold blowing in through the door.

Van pulls back, putting chilly fingers under my chin and forcing my gaze up. "I love you," he says.

"Never doubted it," I assure him. Not once did I ever think he just fell out of love with me.

His smile is lopsided. "I'm an idiot."

"Never doubted that either." I pull back from him. He mentioned something about groveling and I'm going to insist he get on with it.

Van stares at me for a moment, accepting we're at the part of this reunion where he's going to have to humble himself a little. However, it can be done with a cup of cocoa.

I turn for the kitchen and I hear Van grabbing his duffel from the porch before shutting the door. His footsteps are heavy as he stands just inside the kitchen, watching me pour the steaming chocolate from the pot into his favorite mug. I glance at him and I'm relieved to see he doesn't look uncomfortable. No matter how bad these last few weeks have been, I don't want either of us to suffer anymore.

I hand Van his hot chocolate and we move into the living room. I resume my seat on one end of the couch and to my surprise, Van doesn't take the other end. Or even the chair to my right.

He stands on the other side of the coffee table before the fireplace. I wait patiently as he takes a sip of his cocoa and sets the mug up on the mantel before facing me.

"So," he says, spreading his arms as if he has a speech all planned. Except he falters and then his face crumbles, as if he doesn't quite know how to start.

I give him a little push. "How did you even get here? You have a game tomorrow night. Surely you don't intend to drive back because if you do, you're going to need to leave pretty soon."

Van offers a sheepish smile. "I chartered a small jet out of Pittsburgh. Of note, our savings account is about $16,000 light because of that."

I'm shocked by that number because Van is kind of frugal. Despite having millions from his hockey career, he doesn't spend money in flashy ways. Still, it's adorable that he seems chagrined about it.

"How about you tell me why you're here."

"Obviously, because I came to my senses. Max told me I would and I did."

I didn't know Max had talked to Van. "What in the world did he say to you that I haven't over the last few weeks to make you decide to stop being a moron?"

Van shakes his head and moves around the coffee table to sit next to me. He shifts on his hip to angle my way. "He didn't say anything in particular. Just told me things would work out. It was Drake who made things clear to me."

My face puckers in confusion. "Drake?"

"Yeah... I went with him and Boone to the children's hospital this morning, visited with the sick kids—which, as a side note, was absolutely gut-wrenching—but we went out for beers after."

There's no helping the soft hum from my throat. The thought of Van visiting sick kids makes me a gooey mess inside. He hears it and smiles gently, reaching out to take my hand. I don't pull away, instead letting him cradle my fingers as he continues to talk. "Drake's ex-wife is an addict and apparently, it's been pretty tough on his boys. I don't know exactly how old they are, but I saw them once at the arena and they're young. Like seven or so. Anyway, they've seen some shit with her."

"Poor kiddos," I coo, wanting to wrap them in a hug. Drake as well.

"Yeah... poor kiddos, except... they're well-adjusted and happy."

Now I see where he's going with this. "You saw firsthand that kids can face tough things and come out just fine."

"Sort of. I mean, yes... it was validating to hear his advice and he assured me kids are resilient and need transparency and honesty and guidance and with all of that, they can handle all kinds of things. But I had a different sort of epiphany."

I tilt my head. "What's that?"

Van's gaze falls away from me and he rubs his jaw. I feel the guilt radiating off him and I squeeze the hand still entwined with mine. "Van?"

When he turns his regard back to me, his expression is awash with shame. "My epiphany is that I wasn't trying to spare my future children from the pain of my past... I think I was really wanting to spare myself. I didn't see how I could do it. How I could protect them and be a good dad. It felt... insurmountable and I felt weak. I never had a father figure, so I didn't think I had it in me to do right by them."

"Oh," I murmur, glancing down at where our hands are connected. I had not expected that at all. My head lifts. "But you're not weak. You're one of the strongest, most accomplished people I know. You overcame a horrific childhood to become an incredibly successful, kind and loving man. You can do anything you set your mind to, baby."

Van nods. "Yeah... I know. I mean, I'm scared, but you're right. I know I can do this. That was my secondary epiphany after acknowledging my true fear... that I can do this, and with you by my side, it won't be as scary. Drake said it's hard work, but I can do what it takes."

I nod in agreement, but still... Van's first inclination

was to push me away. To abandon our dreams of having kids and I tell him this. "You didn't even try to figure this out with me. You left me."

"And therein lies the true problem… can you forgive me for it? I did it to you once before and I can't one hundred percent guarantee I won't get freaked out again in the future. But the one thing you have to remember, never did I stop loving you. I once told you that I'd never love another soul the way I love yours and that holds true today. If you kick me out of here right now, it will be true in fifty years. Even if you marry someone else and have kids with them, I'll love you until my dying day."

A small breath wafts out of my mouth, but the rest of the air seems trapped in my lungs.

Van leans into me, cups my cheek. "Please say you forgive all the ways I hurt you. Please say you love me the way I love you. Most of all, please tell me that you still want a life with me and that you want to have babies and we can raise them to be strong, fierce children who can handle anything."

Van's eyes are lasered onto mine, his body tensed for me to push him away. Instead, I say, "I'm pregnant."

I watch him carefully because this is where I'll know for sure just how committed he is.

For what seems like forever, his expression is as unyielding as a sculpture. But then something beautiful and miraculous happens. The change is subtle at first... a muscle in his jaw twitches and the corners of his mouth lift as if he's undecided between a smile and a frown. His brows draw inward as he processes those two words I just uttered. Then a spark ignites, dancing across his gorgeous blue irises, and his pupils dilate as if trying to absorb the news I just handed over.

That uncertain smile gets bigger, tentative at first until it takes over his entire face. Relief and joy radiate, but his eyes soften with wonder as he glances down toward my belly. I pull his hand and place his palm there.

"We have a baby in there?" he asks in wonder, his voice cracking with emotion.

My heart melts. "We do."

"When?" he asks, then his eyes fly up with fear shining brightly over something new he's considered. "The accident? Is it okay?"

"The baby's fine. They did an ultrasound at the hospital."

"Oh God, Simone." Van falls forward onto me, laying his head in my lap, and while I can't see his face, I can hear the tears in his voice. "I should have been there for you. I should have been by your side every step of the way."

I pet his head, whispering soothing words. "It's okay. You're here now."

"Why didn't you tell me?" he asks, lifting to stare at me. I'm surprised there's no condemnation, just curiosity.

"I wanted you to want this baby, not be obligated to it. I didn't want to get you back that way."

Van nods, his gaze drifting toward the fire in contemplation. "How can you trust that I'm here for the right reasons, then?"

His focus remains on the fire, as if he's afraid to look at me when I provide the answer. I reach out a hand, slide it behind his neck and force him to face me. "Because I trust you love me, Van. That is something that was never once damaged in all of this craziness. Not once did I question your love or your loyalty. In fact, I know it was the depth of your love that had you acting crazy."

Van's expression is dubious, so I bring our faces closer as I repeat the words he needs. "I trust your love for me."

He just stares, his expression doubtful.

"Do you hear me? Do you believe me?" I press, squeezing his neck.

"I always believe everything you tell me," he murmurs. "You're the one person who I know will always give it to me straight."

"And you know I love you, right?"

"You must to even let me in the door," he says dryly.

"I love you more than anything, Van."

And finally, after weeks of wanting him to make a true move that expresses how he feels in actions instead of words, Van takes my face in his palms and kisses me. It's soft and gentle, his lips having immediate mastery over mine. His tongue slips in my mouth, touching my own briefly before he pulls away. Resting his forehead to mine, he says, "We're having a baby."

I hear the excitement in his voice and it's music to my ears. "We're having a baby," I echo.

Van lifts his head and I'm surprised by the desire in his expression. "Is it weird that you being pregnant makes me want to fuck you really bad?"

I snicker and press my mouth to his, giving a slight shake of my head. "Lucky for you, pregnancy hormones make me hornier than normal."

"Jesus… I've died and gone to heaven." Van leans back, his lust quelled a tiny bit as he asks for one more affirmation. "What else do I need to do to make this right?"

"Nothing," I assure him.

"Well, I did bring you something that I was hoping to use to convince you to give me another chance," he says, moving off the couch and rounding to his duffel. I twist to see him rummaging in it and he pulls out a white shirt.

Returning to the couch, he spreads it open and hands

it back to me. I gasp when I see it, then start laughing. It's a Titan Queens T-shirt like the one I cut up.

I reach for it but he jerks it back, wagging a finger. "You only get this if you pack your bags and return to Pittsburgh with me tomorrow morning. You have to act the part of hockey wife if you want the official T-shirt, assuming you want that. I know we have to figure out your job and everything."

Laughing, I throw myself into his arms, knocking him onto the couch. I kiss him hard before saying, "Yes, I'm going back with you."

He grins up at me. "Almost all my dreams have come true."

"What other dream needs to be fulfilled?" I ask as I stroke my fingers over his collarbone.

"I need you to get naked, Simone. I need it bad."

CHAPTER 18

Van

"**V**AN," BOONE CALLS before I'm able to slip out of the locker room. "You better get your ass over to Mario's for a celebratory beer."

"Not tonight. I've got a hot date."

Several of the guys laugh and I throw my hand up in the air to wave goodbye. I spread the word during the pregame prep that Simone and I were back together.

I turn left out of the locker room and make my way over to the family lounge where I find Simone sitting around a table with some of her Titan Queens. I haven't met all the significant others yet, given how I pretty much avoided everyone during my first two weeks with the team. Simone doesn't see me coming, but some of the other women do and nod my way.

Turning in her chair, she catches sight of me and I'm dazzled by the smile she bestows. I'm the luckiest fucking man on earth that she's still in love with me, warts and all. Bending down, I press my mouth to hers for a soft kiss. When we break apart, she introduces me to Stone's fiancée Harlow, Coen's wife Tillie, and I've already met Gage's fiancée Jenna. They're all wearing their Titan Queens T-shirts.

"Where are the rest of your girls?" I ask. Simone sat in the owner's box with Brienne and her new posse to watch our win over the Washington Breakers.

"Already headed over to Mario's with their menfolk," Simone replies. "You ready to go?"

"More than ready." I hold out my hand to Simone and she uses it to stand from her chair. Turning back to her friends, she bids them good night and blows a kiss with promises to hang out at the next home game.

Simone and I mutually agreed to go home after the game, wanting instead to be alone. The past few weeks have been horrible for both of us, but Simone deserved none of it. I want to spend the night worshipping her—physically and emotionally. I want to fuck our brains out and then I want us to stay up all night talking about all the things we need to do for the baby.

She yawns as we head to the players' lot in the garage. I know she's exhausted, given our escapades after we made up last night at our home in Vermont, only for us to catch an early charter flight back to Pittsburgh so I could get to the arena. Add on a three-hour stint for the game and I'm thinking maybe I should just tuck her into bed.

I hold her hand the entire trip home, resting it on my

thigh.

"Did Etta ever call you back?" she asks.

Chuckling, I nod. "I had to do some groveling, as expected." I called my aunt first thing this morning to let her know that Simone and I were going to be just fine, and then we ended up playing a little bit of phone tag as it was a game day. "Then I had to listen to her berate me for what I did to you and of course, I took it. I deserved it."

"You kind of did," Simone admits with a sheepish grin.

"It's a testament to how much Etta loves you. I swear I think she would have disowned me if I didn't make things right."

"No way," Simone says with a squeeze to my hand. "She loves you far too much."

We're silent a moment, then I can't help but ask. "And the Fournier clan?"

Simone snorts. "I didn't talk to them. I just sent a group text that said we were back together, everything was fine and unless they wanted to incur my wrath they'd forgive you and treat you well."

"It will be fine," I assure her, although I wouldn't put it past Lucas to make me do some extra sucking up to him.

Once we get home, Simone slips into the master bathroom while I get undressed, hanging my suit in the closet. Yeah… tonight I should let her get a good night's sleep. I can fuck her in the morning and then we can talk about the baby over breakfast.

I'm just pulling back the covers on the bed when the bathroom door opens and Simone is standing there wearing one of her skimpy negligees that has me about swallowing my tongue. It's cream-colored and made of a sheer material that hides nothing. I can see her nipples and her pussy through the little night dress, and my cock starts to lengthen.

I'm frozen as she moves to the opposite side of the bed and then crawls across it toward me. Her breasts sway and she licks at her lower lip. Going to her knees, she slides her hands up my chest and over my shoulders to lace behind my neck. "Hi," she whispers.

"Hey, baby." My hands slide under the dress to rest on her bare hips and my thumbs stroke back and forth over her silky skin. My gaze roams over her face. "You are so fucking beautiful."

Lifting one hand, I bring it up to her head and run my fingers through her long hair. She purrs and leans into me.

"As sexy as this little nightie is, I'm going to dispense with it," I announce as I pull it up and over her head, letting it float to the ground.

"You going to take these off?" Simone asks, her fingers tugging playfully at my briefs.

She doesn't have to ask twice. I pull back from her for two seconds to slide them down my legs and kick them away. Simone's hand wraps around my stiff cock, and I groan as she bends forward to run her tongue along its length.

Wrapping her hair in my hand, I tug her upward and away from my dick. Without releasing my hold, I lean back so I can take her in. She's on her knees, legs spread slightly and chest heaving with pebbled nipples. With my other hand, I drag my knuckles over the lips of her sex.

Simone shudders and I drop my gaze downward, watching as I twist my hand to press a finger into her. "Oh, baby… you are soaked already."

"Can't help it if I want you," she murmurs.

I withdraw my finger, rubbing the wetness over her bottom lip. "Kiss me, Simone."

Her hands to my face, she touches those sweet lips against mine in a gentle graze before claiming my mouth. I groan at the taste of mint toothpaste and her sex swirling over my tongue.

It seems like forever we just make out, tongues dueling and my fingers playing in lazy strokes between her legs.

Moving my mouth to her jaw, I ask, "What's going through your mind right now, baby?"

"That I'm going to die if you don't fuck me soon,"

she complains.

Chuckling, I ease her onto the bed and bring my body down on top of hers. Simone's legs part and wrap around my back as I take her mouth again, this time deeply before moving to tiny nibbles against her lips and along her neck. My cock aches as it presses against her wet heat, but I'm not ready to lose myself inside her just yet.

I want to drive her out of her mind first.

Lifting my torso, I work my mouth down her neck and over her breasts, licking and sucking at her nipples. Simone's fingers thread through my hair as I move down her body. When I reach her tummy, I press a kiss there and whisper, "Hi, baby... please ignore what me and your mommy are doing right now."

I glance up and find my wife watching me with the sweetest smile tinged with awe.

"What?" I demand. "I'm going to talk to our kid all the time. Get used to it."

"You're going to be the best dad," she whispers.

"Right now, I want to be the best husband, so be quiet and let me do my job."

Simone sinks into the mattress and spreads her legs wide for me.

"Going to make you feel so good," I promise just before I close my mouth over her pussy. Simone's hips buck, but I hold her down. Nipping at the inside of her thigh, I say, "Keep still or I won't let you come."

She huffs out an exasperated breath, but I know if I were to look up at her, she's smirking. I lick at her clit with teasing, gentle circles, sometimes running my tongue up her center. And fuck, does she taste good.

"Van," Simone pleads, her hips trying to gyrate for more friction. I lift my head and find her staring at me with wild eyes. "Will you just make me come so you can fuck me?"

"No, I don't think I will. I think I'm going to edge you all night—"

"You better not," she warns.

Laughing darkly, I rest my chin just above her pelvis and wait until her head lifts so her eyes meets mine. "You're not in the driver's seat, baby. I am. Are we clear?"

Simone attempts a glare, but I know her too well. That's excitement etched all over her face because my wife loves to be dominated in bed. Flopping back down with a huff, she mutters, "Fine."

Yes, very fine. "Now I've got to start all over," I tease.

It's with nibbling kisses inside her thighs and barely-there strokes of my fingers along the lips of her pussy. I circle my tongue around her clit and gently press a finger inside her before pulling it out ever so slowly. Simone makes tiny, strangled noises and does her best to keep those hips from moving. Her thighs are shaking and her breathing turns ragged, but my sweet girl stays still and takes it like I knew she could.

"Want to come?" I ask her.

"Yes, please," she moans.

"All right, baby… you can give it to me now." I thrust two fingers inside and curl them, causing her to groan. I purse my lips around her clit and suck hard.

Simone splinters, screaming out my name. Her hips buck hard, catching me in the chin, and I chuckle as I continue to lap at her. "Mmm… that's my good girl."

Fingers sliding into my hair, Simone jerks hard at me… her demand that I move north and give her more.

I kiss my way up her body, whispering hello to the kid as I pass her belly. Simone reaches in between our bodies, her hand fisting my cock, and she's not joking that she wants it now. Her other hand comes to my ass and she pulls on me hard, attempting to guide me into her body. I'm still stronger than she is and I don't budge, instead dropping my face to hers. "Kiss me first and tell me how good you taste on my mouth."

Simone's eyes flash with lust and she runs her tongue over my lower lip before kissing me so deep I see stars.

I pull away and tether my gaze to her gorgeous face. "Tell me you love me."

"I love you, baby. Always. Never going to change."

"Never," I agree as I press my hips forward, finding exactly where I need to be and slide my cock deep inside her pussy.

"Fuck," I groan, pressing my forehead to hers and holding still for just a second to get my bearings.

Simone's fingers play lightly at my hip, waiting for me to move. She lifts her head, runs her lips along my neck. Even those delicate touches from her have my balls tingling.

I press my palms into the mattress and raise my torso so I can look down at my wife. Our eyes lock and hold as I start to move inside her. Simone bites into her lower lip and I let my gaze divert just for a bit to look down between our bodies. I fucking love watching my dick tunneling in and out of her, laying claim to all that is mine.

I roll my hips, pressing deeper into her body. Simone gasps and I grab her hand, shove it between us until her fingertips are at her clit. "Make yourself come again, baby."

"Okay," she huffs out as her legs spread wider for me.

I grind down into her, thrusting harder as I can feel the very edge of my orgasm brewing.

Faster and faster, the hard punches of my hips banging the bed into the wall.

"More," Simone rasps, her breath stuttering in ragged bursts through her full lips.

I put my hand on the back of her thigh, lift that leg higher and go in for an even deeper angle. My first thrust in and Simone is screaming, her back arching off the bed and her body stiffening in a choke hold of an orgasm that I feel rippling all around my cock.

It's just the sort of thing that drives a man like me crazy, watching my wife clawed apart by the pleasure I give her. It's enough to throw me over the edge and I slide in to the hilt one last time, close my eyes as I groan out an orgasm so intense, I think I might have just impregnated my wife again.

I drop down onto Simone, holding most of my weight off her. Our bodies are slick with sweat and I feel my pulse thumping in my neck.

"Damn," Simone whispers. "You outdid yourself, honey."

I can barely breathe, but I manage to brush my lips against hers in silent agreement.

Rolling us to our sides so I don't crush her, I pull Simone in close to me. Our legs remain tangled and I run my fingertips up her spine as we lie there silently. I'm so fucking mellow I could sleep right now, and I know we both need it.

"Van?" Simone murmurs, her breath wafting across my chest.

"Mmm?"

"Will it always be this way between us?"

She's talking about our insane sexual chemistry. It was explosive from the first time we kissed and it hasn't lessened in the years we've been together. Except for the clusterfuck I've made of the last two weeks, my wife has given me pleasure that I'm confident most people could never hope to achieve. She's the only one who rocks my world and I'll never get tired of this.

"Always," I assure her.

"We'll have to make time for this after the baby comes."

Mellow mood evaporating, I lift my head to look down at her. Not because this upsets or worries me, but because it intrigues me. "Why's that?"

Simone giggles. "Because babies are a lot of work. And we're going to lose sleep and we'll be too tired to fuck."

"Yeah, that's not ever happening," I say with confidence, but then my smile turns soft. "Tell me more stuff about babies. What's our new life going to be like?"

"Hmm," she says as if pondering where to start. "Well, one thing I read was that dads get to change all the poopy diapers since moms have the task of breast-feeding."

"I don't believe that for a second." I laugh and then roll her to her back. I scoot down the bed and rest my cheek on her stomach, facing her. I know I can't feel or hear anything, but it fills me with such wonder that a tiny person is growing in there. I stroke Simone's skin and press my lips just below her belly button. "Hey, baby... are you going to be a boy or a girl? I'm hoping for a girl and I'm not sure why. I think because I want to spoil you the way I spoil your mom. And I hope you come out just like her, even her bratty attitude, because your mom is the best person I know and the world will be better with two like you in it."

On a sniffling sound, I twist to find Simone crying. She wipes at the tears and smiles down at me. "Don't stop," she says. "Keep talking."

Her hand comes to my head and she strokes my hair as I tell our kid all the wonderful things that await her in this world when she arrives.

Boone Rivers uses his fame and fortune as a professional hockey player to his advantage, but not in the way most people would think. Volunteering as often as his busy schedule will allow, Boone meets one brave young boy who turns his world upside down. GO HERE to get all the details on Boone!

sawyerbennett.com/bookstore/boone

Nestled within the lush, rolling hills of Kentucky, among its proud horse farms and ancient bourbon distilleries, the Blackburn and Mardraggon families' bloodline conflict runs deep and without forgiveness. Prepare to get swept away with this series of seductive romance standalones rife with high drama and entwined with the bitter rivalry between these two dynasties. GO HERE for all the details on the Bluegrass Empires series!

sawyerbennett.com/book-series/bluegrass-empires

Go here to see other works by Sawyer Bennett:

https://sawyerbennett.com/bookshop

Don't miss another new release by Sawyer Bennett!!! Sign up for her newsletter and keep up to date on new releases, giveaways, book reviews and so much more.

https://sawyerbennett.com/signup

Connect with Sawyer online:

Website: sawyerbennett.com

Twitter: twitter.com/bennettbooks

Facebook: facebook.com/bennettbooks

Instagram: instagram.com/sawyerbennett123

Goodreads: goodreads.com/Sawyer_Bennett

Amazon: amazon.com/author/sawyerbennett

BookBub: bookbub.com/authors/sawyer-bennett

About the Author

New York Times, USA Today, and Wall Street Journal Bestselling author Sawyer Bennett uses real life experience to create relatable stories that appeal to a wide array of readers. From contemporary romance, fantasy romance, and both women's and general fiction, Sawyer writes something for just about everyone.

A former trial lawyer from North Carolina, when she is not bringing fiction to life, Sawyer is a chauffeur, stylist, chef, maid, and personal assistant to her very adorable daughter, as well as full-time servant to her wonderfully naughty dogs.

If you'd like to receive a notification when Sawyer releases a new book, sign up for her newsletter (sawyerbennett. com/signup).

Printed in the USA
CPSIA information can be obtained
at www.ICGtesting.com
CBHW051948011223
2280CB00020B/135